Will Sky miss out on the fun?

"I think this calls for some kind of celebration," Alex said, leaning back in her chair.

"Alex is right," Carrie stated. "We *should* celebrate. Jordan deserves a reward."

For a second, Carrie and Jordan just stared at each other. Then their eyes began to widen. Smiles spread across their faces.

Sky's gaze kept shifting between the two of them. Okay, something weird was going on here. . . .

"Wild World!" they both cried at the same time.

Sky blinked, totally bewildered. "*What* world?"

"Wild World," Jordan repeated. "It's a brand-new jumbo amusement park with forty roller coasters," he explained breathlessly.

Sky's heart immediately began to sink. If Wild World was an amusement park, there was no way she'd be able to go. A day at an amusement park probably cost at least thirty bucks—if not a lot more. So Jordan and Carrie could count her out of the celebration.

"Oh, man," Jordan murmured. "This is gonna be awesome."

"Yeah," Sky echoed hollowly. "Awesome."

Face Facts, Sky

M·a·k·i·n·g F·r·i·e·n·d·s

Face Facts, Sky

Kate Andrews

This paperback edition published in 1999.

First published in 1997 by Macmillan Children's Books.
Reprinted by arrangement with William Morrow & Company.

Photography by Jutta Klee.

Printed in Canada.
10 9 8 7 6

Skyler Foley's
Biggest Confession Ever

So, I was thinking that maybe I should become a writer like Carrie. I know, it sounds ridiculous. But Carrie wrote a story that won a prize—about a girl named Mercedes who thought she was hiding a deep, dark secret from everyone—and I feel like I could have written the same thing.

That's because I know what it's like to keep a major secret from your best friends. It's almost impossible. In fact, I bet most of my friends would say that *my* biggest secret isn't even a secret at all.

My biggest secret?

It's pretty simple, really—my family doesn't have much money.

Yeah, I know. It doesn't take a genius to figure that out.

Still, nobody knows just how bad things really are.

Let me give you an example. I bring my own lunch to school, right? I'm the only one of my friends who does that. Robert Lowell Middle School doesn't even <u>like</u> it when people bring their own lunches. They only allow it in certain cases. Like mine.

That's because my parents don't have the money to pay for the regular school lunch.

Or how about this? I know everyone always makes fun of how much I go to the mall. They think that's the only place I want to hang out. But do you know why I really spend so much time there? Because I love clothes. And the only way I can get what I want is to wait until it goes on sale, then grab it.

So, it's not like I really feel like hanging out at the mall all the time. But how else am I ever going to be able to get the stuff I want? It's not like I can just walk in and buy whatever I see.

Another example is the Foley family spring "vacation." Every spring my parents take our boat on a little trip up the Pacific Coast to Canada. The only reason we do it is because it doesn't cost anything. We can't afford to go on a <u>real</u> vacation. But my friends don't know that. They actually think it's <u>cool</u>. That I'm so lucky my family has so much fun together.

Yeah, real lucky. Every day, I go through life pretending that, just like my hippie parents, I don't care about material stuff. Pretending that I'm not broke.

It's just one more way that I feel <u>different</u> from all my friends.

The thing is, I probably should be used to feeling

different by now. I mean, no one ever talks about it or anything, but my parents have a mixed marriage. My dad is African-American, and my mom isn't.

But that's another story.

Maybe I shouldn't become a writer, after all. I could never write anything good enough to win a contest like Carrie did. Then again, she did win a hundred-dollar gift certificate, just for telling a story. . . .

One

"Hey, Jordan," Alex Wagner whispered, digging her spoon into a yellowish blob that was supposed to be some kind of dessert pudding. "Don't look now, but The Amys are staring at you again."

Jordan just moaned, then slouched down in his chair. Strands of unruly blond hair immediately covered his face.

Poor guy, Sky thought. She'd never felt really, really sorry for Jordan Sullivan until now. But he was so nervous he actually looked *sick*. There were dark circles under his droopy blue eyes, and the rest of his skin had turned a color not too different from the pudding.

Then again, he had every right to look sick. He'd made fools out of The Amys—Amy Anderson, Aimee Stewart, and Mel Eng—the three most popular and influential girls at Robert Lowell Middle School. No one ever did something to The Amys without suffering some kind of ugly retaliation.

Sky was kind of surprised that something awful hadn't happened to Jordan already. The Amys usually struck quickly. Of course, it was only

10

Monday. And the rest of the long afternoon still loomed ahead.

"I gotta hand it to you, Jordan," Carrie Mersel murmured. She tucked a few strands of her dyed black hair behind one ear, then shot a quick glance at The Amys' lunch table. Her hazel eyes flashed wickedly. "They are really, really mad."

"You know, Jordan," Sam Wells whispered, giving his spiky black hair a thoughtful scratch. "If I were you, I'd keep a low profile."

"I know," Jordan groaned. "You don't have to remind me."

Sky shook her head. She still couldn't get over how Jordan had been so . . . well, selfless. Usually, he was too busy doodling on his sketch pad or making dumb wisecracks to really think about helping someone out of a jam. But he had made the ultimate sacrifice for Carrie. When her short story had won a prize and she'd been asked to do a reading in public, Jordan had come up with a brilliant plan to keep The Amys occupied so they wouldn't show up and embarrass Carrie. It was amazing.

"So?" Alex whispered. She leaned so far forward that her shoulder-length brown hair was almost dangling in her food. "How'd you do it?"

"It wasn't that hard," Jordan finally mumbled. His eyes kept darting over to The Amys' table. "I just convinced my brother Paul that Mel was one of Amy Anderson's sisters."

Sky thought for a second. Wasn't that impossible? For one thing, the Anderson sisters were all blonde—and Mel was Chinese. "How'd you do *that?*" she asked.

Jordan shrugged. "Well, Paul knows that Amy Anderson has two sisters, but in his typically stupid Paul way, he didn't know what their names were. And he never saw Mel before. So I told him that Mel was Amy's second-oldest sister. I told him to call her at the Andersons'. I picked a time when I knew she was going to be there."

Carrie raised her eyebrows. "Let me guess. During *Days of Our Lives?*" The Amys never missed their favorite soap opera, even on weekends. Every Sunday at noon the three girls gathered at the Andersons' house to watch a videotape of the past week's episodes.

Jordan nodded. A sly grin crossed his face. "Exactly. I also told Paul that Mel had a crush on him."

Sky made a face. The thought of Paul and Mel as a couple . . . "Eww!" she whispered, unable to control herself.

"Anyway, she knew who she was talking to, but he didn't," Jordan continued. "See, Mel really thought that Paul liked her. And Paul thought he was talking to someone named Mel Anderson, who liked *him.* They talked for ten whole minutes."

"Wow," Carrie murmured. "Your brothers really are stupid."

Jordan shrugged again. "I've been telling you that for years."

"Wait—so how did you convince the rest of them?" Sky asked. "I mean, what about Amy and Aimee and your other two brothers?"

"That's the lucky part," he said in a low voice. He leaned forward a little. "See, I told Paul that I overheard Amy's sisters talking. And I told him that I knew they wanted to do something on Sunday afternoon. So Paul asked Mel if he could come over on Sunday. And Mel said, 'Sure—but bring your brothers. There are three of us.' And that was that."

Sky shook her head in disbelief. "Man," she whispered after a moment. "Your brothers must have *freaked* when they saw The Amys. That is . . ."

"Genius," Carrie finished for her. "Pure genius."

"Genius?" Sam joked, cocking his eyebrow. "I don't know about that."

Sky laughed. Sam was the only one besides her who ever kept Jordan in line. It was a good thing, too. Jordan was the type of guy who would actually start to *believe* he was a genius if he heard it enough times.

"You know, I almost feel bad for calling you Jor-*dumb* all these years," Sky said. She flashed Jordan a wide smile.

"Thanks, Sky," Jordan muttered sarcastically.

"Well, I think this calls for some kind of celebration," Alex said, leaning back in her chair. "I mean, this was huge. We should, you know . . . what's the word? . . . enjoy, but more . . ." She began snapping her fingers.

"Savor?" Carrie suggested.

"Exactly." Alex nodded. "We should savor it before it's too late."

Jordan laughed dismally. "You mean before my brothers kill me?"

Alex's grin disappeared. "Actually, I was thinking more about The Amys," she said.

"Either way," Jordan groaned, "I'm dead."

"Oh, come on," Sky said, patting him on the back. "It's not that bad. We'll protect you."

"Well, let's not worry about that now," Carrie stated. "I think Alex is right. I think we *should* celebrate. Jordan deserves a reward."

Jordan rolled his eyes. "Carrie, you already gave me a reward. You gave me one hundred bucks worth of comic books. That's more than I deserve."

"I was thinking more about doing something we could all enjoy together," Carrie said.

For a second, Carrie and Jordan just stared at each other. Then their eyes began to widen. Smiles spread across their faces.

Sky's gaze kept shifting between the two of them. Okay, something weird was going on here. . . .

"Wild World!" they both cried at the same time.

Sky blinked, totally bewildered. "*What* world?"

"Wild World," Jordan repeated. He looked shocked. "You've never heard of it?"

Sky shook her head.

Carrie's eyes narrowed. "Wait, Sky . . . you haven't been living in one of those experimental airtight bubbles or anything, have you?" she teased.

"Wild World is a brand-new jumbo amusement park with forty roller coasters," Jordan explained breathlessly.

"Oh, yeah!" Alex suddenly exclaimed. "I saw the commercial last night. It just opened last weekend. It's got a skateboard park and a virtual reality tent and . . ."

Sky's heart immediately began to sink. No wonder she hadn't heard of it. In a way, her houseboat was like an airtight bubble. Her parents never kept any normal newspapers or magazines around the house, and her TV only got two channels. Anyway, if Wild World was an amusement park, there was no way she'd be able to go. A day at an amusement park probably cost at least thirty bucks—if not a lot more. So Jordan and Carrie could count her out of the celebration.

"What's the matter?" Alex asked.

"Uh . . . no-nothing," Sky stammered. "It's just that, uh, I just remembered something," she lied. "I have to check with my parents first. You know, I think they have some kind of family outing planned next weekend." *And it's definitely something that doesn't cost thirty bucks per person*, she added silently.

"Well, I'm sure they'd let you get out of it to come with us," Carrie said reassuringly. "Your parents are usually so cool about stuff like that."

"Usually," Sky mumbled.

"Hey—doesn't Wild World have a big wave pool?" Sam asked. His black eyes were glistening with excitement. "You know, the one that's the size of a small lake?"

Jordan nodded. "Totally. I mean, you could surf on it. I read an article that said the waves get up to ten feet tall. . . ."

Sky tried to listen as Jordan jabbered on and on about the wave pool, but eventually she couldn't take it anymore. It was too depressing. She could picture exactly what would happen when she got home. She would beg and plead and fight with her parents to let her go to Wild World . . . and they would just smile their mellow smiles and say: "You can go some other time, Sky. Things are a little tight right now."

That's what they always said whenever she wanted to do something that involved money.

The thing was, there wouldn't be any other time. There was never any other time. And it was pretty clear now that Carrie and Jordan and Alex and Sam had made up their minds. They were going to go to Wild World this weekend and they were going to have a great time. Period. By the sound of things, they were practically there already.

"Oh, man," Jordan murmured. "I hope I can survive the week. If my brothers or The Amys don't kill me, this is gonna be awesome."

"Yeah," Sky echoed hollowly. "Awesome."

Two

By the time Bus #4 dropped Sky in front of the little dock that led to her houseboat, she was frantic. She *had* to go to Wild World. It was something she couldn't miss out on. Listening to her best friends ramble on all day about go-carts and water slides and rides that turned you upside down until you wanted to vomit . . . well, it had been more than she could handle.

To top it all off, Jordan and Carrie had figured out that the trip would probably cost about fifty bucks per person. *Fifty.* Sky still couldn't believe it. And as if that wasn't bad enough, no one seemed worried about how they'd come up with the money. Sam had said he'd just mow the neighbors' lawn in addition to his family's. Jordan announced he'd been saving up for some new comics, but that this trip would be just as good. Alex said she could ask for an advance on the allowance she got for helping her dad out around the house. And Carrie was quite sure her parents would just hand her the whole fifty bucks. Sky knew they would, too. The whole thing was enough to make her dizzy.

And how would she, Sky, get the money? Well . . . she would just have to talk her parents into giving it to her. It was that simple. She'd even made a little list of arguments during Ms. Lloyd's English class.

<u>Why You Should Let Me Go to Wild World</u>

1. Last year you forgot to sign my permission slip for the class trip to the Seattle Aquarium, so you owe me a fun trip.
2. Jordan may get killed by The Amys or his brothers, so it's important that I spend as much quality time with him as possible.
3. I can bring leftovers to school for lunch instead of using fresh food, which will save money.
4. I can skip lunch one day a week, which will save money.
5. I'll give up going to the mall for a while. (Use only if all other arguments fail.)

Sky paused on the dock. She pulled the list from her jeans pocket and glanced at it one last time. The little scrap of paper flapped in the breeze. Her hands were moist and shaky. This would never work. She'd made this list when she still thought the trip would cost only thirty dollars.

"Sky?" her mom called.

Sky looked up with a start. Before she knew it, the paper had slipped from her fingers. She watched helplessly as a gust of wind carried it far from the dock, then dropped it gently into the blue-gray water of Puget Sound.

Oh, brother.

"What was that, sweetie?" her mom asked, poking her head out the front door of the main cabin. "It wasn't something important, was it?"

Sky shook her head miserably.

"Well, that's good." She paused. "It was paper, right?"

"Yeah, Mom," Sky groaned.

Mrs. Foley smiled. Her long blonde hair fluttered across her face. "Don't worrry, then, Sky," she said. "Paper is biodegradable, so it won't hurt the environment." She disappeared back into the boat.

Sky shook her head again, but she had to laugh. Only her mom would assume that Sky would get so upset over what a scrap of paper would do to the *environment.* The breeze picked up. Sky shivered once. Well, there was no point in waiting out here any longer. It was time to get that fifty bucks.

Get ready, Sky commanded herself. She took a deep breath and clenched her fists at her sides, then marched determinedly through the houseboat door.

"Mom, I . . ." She paused.

Mrs. Foley looked as if she were getting ready to leave. For one thing, she had her "purse"—a frayed old cloth sack that she had gotten in South America or somewhere. It was hideously ugly. In fact, Sky had no idea why her mom didn't just throw it overboard. If anything was biodegradable, it was that . . . *thing*. It had pretty much disintegrated already.

"Did you say something, sweetie?" Mrs. Foley mumbled, smiling distractedly. She was searching through the pillows of the overstuffed brown couch—which meant, of course, that she had lost her car keys.

"Where are you going?" Sky asked.

"Hi, Sky!" Mr. Foley called from belowdecks.

"Hi, Dad," she answered automatically.

Mrs. Foley shook her head. "I want to run a few errands before Leif gets home." She stood up and sighed. "But I can't find—"

"The car keys," Sky finished for her. "I know. Listen, I'll help you find them in a second. But first there's something I want to talk about with you and Dad."

Mrs. Foley turned her eyes to Sky. "It's not something serious, is it?" she asked, sounding concerned.

Sky managed a smile. "Don't worry. It's nothing *bad*. But it is important."

Her father's heavy footsteps pounded up the steep, narrow staircase from the bedrooms down below. "Hey, there," he sang out cheerfully, stepping into the main cabin.

For a moment, Sky wondered if he had been sleeping. His graying beard and dreadlocks looked vaguely unkempt—and he was barefoot, dressed only in some old cut-off shorts and a T-shirt. But she wouldn't be surprised if he had been taking a nap. He was a writer and did most of his writing in the early morning.

"Did I hear you say you wanted to talk about something?" he asked.

Sky nodded. She glanced between the two of them, twirling her hair around her finger.

"So . . . ?" he urged.

Sky held her breath, then blurted: "Can I have fifty dollars to go to an amusement park this weekend with Carrie and Alex and Jordan and Sam?"

Her father burst out laughing.

Sky hung her head. That was definitely not the response she'd been hoping for. "What's so funny?" she muttered under her breath.

Mr. Foley's laughter faded. "I'm sorry, Sky," he said, giving her hair a playful tussle. "From the way you looked, I thought you were going to tell us that you robbed a bank or something."

Sky made a face. "That's not a bad idea."

Her father sighed. "Sky, you know we can't afford to give you fifty dollars right now—"

"Why not?" she demanded, glaring at him. She'd known all along that this would happen, but she still couldn't help but get angry. She wasn't even angry at her parents. She was just angry at everything. She was angry at her life. "Give me one good reason, okay?"

"The reason is that we don't have it," her mom said gently. "If we did, we'd let you go."

"But you do have it!" Sky protested. "I mean, you have money to buy three different kinds of shampoo—one for Dad, one for you, and one for Leif and me—right?"

"That's different, sweetie—you know it is," Mr. Foley said. "Shampoo is something we need."

"No, it isn't," Sky groaned. "Nothing terrible would happen if we all used the same shampoo for a few months."

"That's true, Sky," her mother said. Her bright green eyes softened. "But that would mean that the whole family would have to make a sacrifice for your benefit. And that's not fair, is it?"

"Why not?" Sky countered. "I make sacrifices for you guys all the time. Who watched Leif when you went to see that lame sixties band this summer?"

Her mother smiled. "I know. Sometimes when you're a kid, life seems unfair."

"What?" Sky spluttered. That had to be the dumbest thing she had ever heard in her life. "You used to do fun stuff all the time when you were a kid!" she cried. She jerked a finger at the biodegradable purse thingy dangling from her mom's shoulder. "I mean, you went all the way to South America!"

23

"Guatemala," her mom corrected. "That's Central America, sweetie."

Sky rolled her eyes. "Whatever. The point is, your parents let you do what you wanted when—"

"Sky, listen to me," her mom interrupted softly. "There's no way you can compare going to an amusement park with going to Central America."

"Why not?" Sky demanded.

Mrs. Foley laughed—which only made Sky even angrier.

"Well, for one thing, I was twenty years old when I went," she said. "So I wasn't exactly a kid like you. Anyway, it was part of a college program. I had to earn the money for that trip myself. It was a learning experience." She paused. "I don't know if going to an amusement park qualifies as a learning experience."

Sky opened her mouth, but she knew right then it was hopeless. No matter what she said, she wasn't going to get that fifty dollars.

"I'm too young to earn the money myself," she finally muttered—as if that meant anything at all.

"I know, sweetheart," her mother replied soothingly. "It's hard. Sometimes you can't participate in all the things you want to. Believe me, I know what that feels like."

She tried to put her arm around Sky's shoulder, but Sky wriggled out from under it.

"You don't know what it feels like," Sky said glumly.

Her mother sighed and gently stroked Sky's hair.

"Listen, Sky—one of these days we'll make it up to you," her father promised. "But right now, we can't give you the money to go to this amusement park. If we did, we'd have to do something with Leif—something just as expensive. And we just can't afford it. Money's too tight right now. It wouldn't be fair to him, and it's not fair to us. So the answer is no."

"And there's nothing I can do to change your minds?" Sky pleaded one last time.

"If we could change our minds, we would, Sky," Mr. Foley said quietly.

Sky stared at him, then at her mother. Their faces looked exactly the same: They had these sad, sympathetic expressions that said, "We're sorry—and we understand perfectly what you must be feeling."

Sky bit her lip to keep from bursting into tears. They didn't understand one bit.

Three

Carrie nearly tripped as she scrambled onto Bus #4. She couldn't remember the last time she had been so psyched. Last night, her mom had gotten tons of amazing information about Wild World off the Internet. Of course, she had only done it to demonstrate the wonders of the information superhighway. Carrie could have cared less about that. But now she had her entire day at the park planned from start to finish.

"Hi, Brick," she said breathlessly as she regained her balance.

"Whoa, there!" the bus driver said. "Careful."

"Very graceful—not!" Amy Anderson called after her.

Carrie paused and smiled over her shoulder. Not even The Amys could spoil her mood today. She was too pumped.

Carrie continued down the aisle and plopped down on the backseat in her usual spot between Jordan and Alex.

"What's up?" Jordan asked, smirking. "You look like you just won the lottery or something."

"Well, I did sort of hit the jackpot," Carrie said. She slung her black backpack onto the floor, right between her combat boots, then yanked a thin stack of folded papers out of the front pocket. "Check this out. My mom got all this stuff about Wild World off the computer. There's all kinds of . . ."

Before she had even finished, Alex, Jordan, and Sam had thrust their hands at her. Carrie rolled her eyes. Within seconds, they had snatched the papers from her and were reading hungrily.

"Anyway, I just hope we have good weather this weekend," Carrie said, sighing. She glanced out the window as the bus bounced down Pike's Way toward Sky's house. The gray sky had been threatening rain all morning. A few fat drops were now splashing on the glass. "You guys can go, right?"

The three of them just grunted.

Carrie grinned. "I'll take that as a 'yes.'"

"Hey—check this out!" Jordan suddenly exclaimed, shoving his paper in Sam's face. "Terror Mountain. It's an indoor roller coaster that's got all these 3-D visual effects."

Sam paused and looked at Carrie curiously. "What kind of printer does your mom have? I've never seen a color photograph this good off a personal printer."

Carrie raised her eyebrows. "You're asking *me* what kind of printer my mom has? How should I know? That's like asking Amy Anderson which company makes the coolest skateboards."

Just then, the bus rolled to a stop in front of Sky's dock. The door squeaked open. Sky climbed on, gave Brick a weak high-five, and began trudging toward the backseat.

Uh-oh, Carrie said to herself. Sky didn't look very thrilled to be there. She didn't make a sound as she squeezed between Carrie and Jordan. Her forlorn brown eyes never rose from the floor.

Carrie was pretty sure that could mean only one thing.

"So, what did your parents say about Wild World?" Carrie asked as hopefully as she could manage.

Sky sighed. The others also must have sensed that the news was going to be bad, because they quickly began folding their papers and stuffing them in their pockets.

"I . . . uh . . . I have to baby-sit Leif this weekend," Sky said slowly. "My parents are going to be out of town and I have to take Leif on a fishing trip. They have it all planned out," she added, glancing at the four of them.

"Well, why don't we just take Leif with us?" Carrie suggested brightly.

"Yeah!" Alex exclaimed. She pulled the crumpled paper out of her baggy jeans pocket. "I just saw that they're having a big grand-opening special." Her eyes flickered over the page. "Here it is. Kids under twelve get in for half price until noon—"

"Leif really wants to go fishing," Sky interrupted. "He couldn't stop talking about it all night."

Carrie's eyes briefly met Jordan's. She could tell that she and Jordan were thinking the same thing: Sky's voice didn't sound normal. It was almost as if she wasn't telling the truth.

"But look, I don't care," Sky continued hastily. "I mean, it's no big deal." She glanced at the four of them again—but her eyes didn't linger on any one face for more than a split second. "A lot of those rides make me totally ill, anyway."

"Are you sure?" Alex asked. "I bet if we told Leif about it, he'd change his mind. Leif's always up for doing new stuff."

"And we don't mind having him along, if that's what you're worried about," Sam added. "It evens out the boy–girl ratio."

Sky didn't say anything.

Carrie knew right then that Sky was hiding something. Sky was never at a loss for words, especially at times like these. She was by far the most chatty of the bunch. And worst of all, Carrie was certain that whatever Sky was hiding was making her depressed. The downward curve of her lips made that painfully clear.

"That's not it," Sky said after a moment. "Really. I'm serious. I don't mind. You guys have fun, all right? I'll go . . . next time."

Carrie studied Sky's sad expression closely.

But Sky just turned toward Carrie and gave her a reassuring smile. "I'll go next time, Carrie," she murmured. "I promise."

<u>Alex Wagner's Book of Deep Thoughts</u>

<u>Entry 8</u>

Okay — call me overly suspicious, but I'm almost positive that Sky isn't telling the truth about this weekend. Why?

Well, for one thing, she says that she has to take Leif on a "fishing trip." I've known Sky for almost eight years now, and she's never, ever had to take her little brother on a fishing trip. Waterskiing, maybe, but never fishing. The Foleys don't even eat fish. They're all strict vegetarians. It just doesn't make sense.

The other thing that doesn't make sense is how she acted the rest of the day. She was really quiet — even during lunch. She hardly even smiled at all. It was totally un-Sky-like. Something is bothering her. Something big.

See, normally Sky is so open. She always says what's on her mind. In a way, that's the coolest thing about her. She never puts on an act about anything — unlike every other single person at Robert Lowell Middle School. (And yes, I admit, that includes me sometimes.)

I guess that's why Sky is the one person who keeps us all so close as friends. Not that she tries to be the boss or anything like that—but she's always there to help out whenever any of us get into a fight. And she always wants us to do things as a group.

So why would she say that she "doesn't mind" missing out on Wild World? That's like Jordan saying he "doesn't mind" getting beaten up by his brothers. It's impossible. If there's one thing Sky can't stand, it's missing out on something that the rest of us are doing.

Four

"Does anyone want carrot sticks and hummus?" Sky called from inside the boat.

Hummus? Alex looked at Carrie. The two of them were crowded next to Jordan and Sam against the rail of the back deck of the Foleys' houseboat, staring into the muddy water of the sound. Rain always made the sound look dirty. But at least the drizzle had finally stopped. A crisp breeze was blowing, and the sky was now a cloud-strewn blue. It was pretty much perfect skateboarding weather, as far as Alex was concerned. She kind of wished she was skating right now.

"What is hummus?" Alex finally whispered.

Carrie just shrugged. "Beats me."

"Don't say that word," Jordan choked out, pretending to be sick. He was gripping his stomach and leaning far over the rail, his face twisted in mock agony. "Hummus . . . *Bleah* . . ."

Sam nudged him in the ribs. "Stop it, man," he hissed, but he was giggling. "That's rude."

"Anyone?" Sky called.

"Um . . . no thanks," Carrie answered.

"Okay." Sky ducked out of the little kitchen and stepped onto the deck. "So what do you guys feel like doing?" she asked.

Alex shook her head. Sky's cheerful grin was completely forced. Her lips were smiling, but her eyes had the same dull, glazed look they'd had all day. Alex suspected this little get-together wasn't doing anything to improve Sky's mood. And Alex still wasn't any closer to finding out what was really bothering Sky. None of them were.

"Why don't we go inside and play poker?" Jordan asked, rubbing his hands together greedily. "There's five of us, right?"

Carrie rolled her eyes. "Because poker isn't any fun if you don't gamble."

Jordan grinned. "Who said anything about not gambling?"

"I thought you said you didn't have any money," Alex said, frowning.

"We don't have to use real money," Sam offered. "We could use Monopoly money or pennies or something."

"That's a great idea!" Carrie suddenly exclaimed. She hurried toward the kitchen door.

Alex followed her with a puzzled stare. Where was Carrie going? She sounded way too excited over a game of poker—especially one that involved fake gambling. She normally hated games.

"I'll just go get the Monopoly set," Carrie said

quickly. But before she disappeared into the boat, she jerked her head at Alex. "Come with me," she mouthed silently.

Aha, Alex said to herself. So Carrie had a plan. Alex shot a quick glance at Sky. Luckily, Sky hadn't seen anything. She was just gazing listlessly at the water.

From inside the boat, Carrie called: "The board is in that closet just outside your bedroom, right, Sky?"

"Mm-hmm," Sky mumbled absently.

"Um . . . I'm kind of cold," Alex announced. "Can I borrow a sweater?"

"Sure," Sky said. "Take any one you want. You know where they are."

Alex hurried after Carrie. She was a little cold, actually. Her baggy T-shirt didn't offer much protection against the wind coming off the water. She snaked her way through the kitchen and the main cabin, then carefully stepped down the stairwell that led to three bedrooms and Mr. Foley's office.

Carrie was waiting for her at the bottom, in the narrow hallway.

"You don't believe any of this stuff about the fishing trip, do you?" Carrie whispered the moment Alex hopped off the last step.

Alex shook her head. "No way," she replied. "It's gotta be something else."

They were right outside Leif's bedroom. On the other side of the cramped hallway was Mr. Foley's office. Alex could hear the busy *clackety clack* of fingers on a computer keyboard. A little farther down were the doors to Sky's bedroom, her parents' bedroom, and the closet containing every piece of random junk the Foleys owned, including an old Monopoly set.

"Let's ask Leif what Sky is really doing this weekend," Carrie breathed.

Alex hesitated. Questioning Leif behind Sky's back seemed pretty underhanded. But then again, if Leif told them what was bothering Sky, maybe they could do something about it.

"Come on," Carrie urged. "We'll make him promise not to tell Sky we talked to him." She grinned. "He'll love that."

Alex chewed her lip anxiously—but finally she nodded her agreement.

Carrie tapped lightly on the door. "Leif?" she murmured. "It's Carrie and Alex. Can we come in for a minute?"

There was a *thump* of feet on the floor and a few footsteps, then the door creaked open.

Leif's little head poked through the crack. "What's up?" he croaked, rubbing his eyes.

Carrie placed her finger over her mouth. "Shh," she whispered.

Alex laughed. She couldn't help it. She always

laughed whenever she saw Leif. He had to be the cutest little eight-year-old kid on the planet. He had a mass of golden hair—and the same copper skin and chocolate brown eyes as Sky. Plus, his face was all puffy from sleep.

"Were you taking a nap?" Alex asked.

He nodded confusedly, as if he wasn't sure. "I think so. What time is it?"

"Almost four," Carrie whispered. "Sorry for waking you up. Listen, we have a secret we want to talk to you about. Let us in and we'll tell you what it is."

His eyes narrowed suspiciously. "You guys aren't gonna tickle me, are you?"

Alex started laughing again. "Nooo . . ."

"Promise?" he demanded.

"Promise," Carrie stated, raising her hand.

Leif paused, but eventually he stepped aside. "All right," he said reluctantly. "But don't mess up anything in here. I have everything in special places."

Alex exchanged a quick grin with Carrie. The two of them carefully tiptoed through mounds of action figures, underwear, comic books, and markers. *How could we mess it up?* Alex wondered. Even her room wasn't this sloppy. She sat next to Carrie on the unmade bed.

"Leif—we're gonna ask you something, and you have to promise us you won't tell a soul," Carrie said in a low voice. "Okay?"

Leif sat on a pile of laundry, facing them. "What's the big secret?" he asked eagerly.

Carrie shook her head. "You have to promise before we can tell you."

"Okay, okay—I promise," he said. "What is it?"

"Especially Sky, all right?" Carrie insisted.

"I *promise*," Leif groaned.

Carrie leaned forward. "Are you guys going fishing this weekend?"

Leif frowned. "Are we doing *what*?"

Carrie glanced at Alex, then back at Leif. "Are you and Sky going fishing this weekend?" she repeated.

Leif stared at the two of them as if they were completely nuts. "Why would we do that? Me and Sky don't even eat fish. And I'd never kill one, even if you paid me a million dollars."

Alex sighed. She'd figured all along that Sky had been lying—but somehow proving it made the whole thing all the more painful.

"So what are you guys doing this weekend?" Carrie asked.

Leif started shaking his head. "I'm going to my friend Barry's house on Saturday. What does that have to do with any secret?"

For a moment, Alex and Carrie looked at each other. Alex felt just as confused as Leif. His plans had nothing to do with Sky. So what was Sky doing? Why couldn't she go to Wild World?

"Let me ask you something, Leif," Alex said. "Is Sky in some kind of trouble or something? Are your parents mad at her?"

He shook his head. "I don't think so. . . ."

"Do you know if she mentioned anything to them about Wild World—you know, that new amusement park?" Carrie asked.

"Oh, that," Leif said. "Yeah, she talked to Mom and Dad about it all during dinner last night."

"She did?" Carrie prodded. "Did she want to go?"

Leif shrugged. "Yeah, but Mom and Dad kept saying that they couldn't just pull fifty bucks out of thin air."

Alex's face fell.

So that was why Sky was so miserable. How could they have been so dumb?

Carrie started shaking her head. "Oh, man," she groaned.

Alex felt like throwing herself out of Leif's small porthole and just letting herself sink to the bottom of the sound. What had they been thinking? They should have known that Wild World would be way too expensive for Sky. And now Sky had come up with this lame excuse because she was obviously too ashamed to admit she didn't have the money.

"So what's the secret?" Leif asked.

Alex blinked and glanced at Carrie. She had no idea what to say.

"The secret is that Sky's friends are jerks," Carrie finally answered.

Leif raised his eyebrows. "You guys came all the way down here to tell me that?" He stood up and headed out the door, sighing disappointedly. "You should have just let me sleep."

Five

The solution to Sky's problem didn't occur to Carrie until she was at her rickety old oak desk that night, trying to do some writing.

It was the first time Carrie had ever experienced "writer's block." Her mind felt like a sieve. She just sat there, staring at the blank piece of paper sticking out of her typewriter as the minutes crept slowly past . . . but no fiendish horror story was leaping onto the page. She didn't understand it. Usually when she was depressed, she could write really well. After all, the last time she'd been depressed she'd won a hundred-dollar gift certificate. . . .

One hundred dollars.

You could take two people to Wild World for one hundred dollars.

Carrie snapped upright in her chair. *That's it!*

Sky couldn't go to Wild World because she didn't have the money—and the rest of her friends did. So all they had to do was cover her. Carrie tried to do some quick math. Fifty divided by four was . . .

Hmm. Math was never her strongest subject. Well, they would just invite Alex's brother, too. If Matt came, there would be five of them. Ten bucks apiece. So instead of paying fifty bucks each, they would pay sixty bucks. No big deal, right? That way, Sky could come, too.

It was so easy.

Carrie leaped off her chair, then dashed to the phone on her night table and punched in Alex's number.

After two rings, Matt answered: "Hello?"

"Matt, hey—it's Carrie," she said, flopping onto the bed. "I'm glad you picked up. I have something I want to ask you. Do you—"

"Whoa, whoa," he interrupted. "If this has anything to do with Amy Anderson, the answer is no."

Carrie pursed her lips. "Of course not. I was just wondering . . ." She paused. *Amy Anderson?* "Wait a sec. Why would you think this has something to do with Amy Anderson?"

"Because I know what happened with Amy Anderson and Jordan's brothers last weekend," Matt replied. "And I don't want to end up like Jordan is gonna end up. So I'm not gonna get involved in any of your pranks against Amy Anderson."

"Jeez. It's nice to know you're on our side," Carrie said sarcastically.

"Hey, I'm in high school now," Matt muttered. "I don't do that childish stuff anymore."

Carrie laughed. "Well, don't worry, Mr. Wimp.

You're safe," she teased. "But what I want to know is—do you want to come to Wild World with us this weekend?"

"Will Amy be there?" he asked.

"Matt," Carrie groaned.

He chuckled. "Just kidding. Yeah, Alex already told me about it. I'm in."

"Good," Carrie said. "There's only one thing. Instead of fifty bucks, it's gonna be sixty. Is that cool?"

"I guess," he said. "What's the deal?"

"Alex will explain it to you," Carrie answered quickly. "Is she there?"

"Sure. Hold on." He took the phone away from his mouth and yelled: "Alex!"

A few seconds later, Alex came to the phone. "Hello?"

"I think I've figured out a way for Sky to come with us this weekend," Carrie announced proudly.

There was a pause. "Lemme guess," Alex said, her voice thick with sarcasm. "You found some buried treasure in your backyard."

"No, I'm serious," Carrie insisted. "Listen. All we have to do is come up with fifty bucks, right? So if each of us chips in another ten bucks—including Matt—then we can pay for her."

Alex didn't say anything.

"Well?" Carrie asked into the silence.

"Uh . . . Do you really think she'll go for that?"

Alex muttered into the phone dubiously.

Carrie frowned. "Why wouldn't she?"

"Well, she might get embarrassed," Alex said. "I mean, I thought the whole reason we avoided talking about money all afternoon was because we didn't want to embarrass her. That's why we played go-fish instead of poker. Anyway, if we just suddenly give her fifty bucks out of the blue, she's gonna figure out we talked to Leif, right? And she probably wouldn't be too thrilled about that."

Carrie blinked a few times. She hadn't thought about it that way.

"So what do you think we should do?" Carrie finally asked, feeling a lot less proud than she had about ten seconds earlier.

Alex sighed. "I don't know."

"Well—what if we just gave her the money as an early birthday present or something?" Carrie suggested, refusing to give up. "Her birthday is next month anyway, right?"

"Yeah—but that still won't explain how we found out she didn't have the money in the first place," Alex pointed out.

"We can just say that we guessed," Carrie said. "I mean, we should have figured it out anyway, right? It was totally obvious that Sky was lying. Sky won't get mad if we tell her that. She knows she's the world's worst liar, especially with us."

Alex laughed. "Yeah, I guess you're right about

that. I was actually thinking the same thing myself."

"So what do you say?" Carrie pressed eagerly.

"Well, okay," Alex agreed. "But we have to go about it in a really careful way, all right?"

Carrie nodded triumphantly. "Definitely. Listen, why don't you call Sam and I'll call Jordan. Bring your ten bucks and Matt's ten bucks with you to school tomorrow. We'll collect all the money on the bus in the morning before Sky gets on. Then I'll give it to her when the two of us are alone sometime during the day. That way, we won't make a big scene in front of everyone. How does that sound?"

"Well, okay," Alex said. "If you really think it'll work. . . ."

"I know it'll work," Carrie stated with complete confidence. "Leave it to me."

Wednesday:
Carrie's Brilliant Plan

8:37 A.M. Carrie collects the money from Jordan, Sam, and Alex.

8:41 A.M. Sky boards the bus in a foul mood, having just heard the long-range weather forecast on the radio. The temperature is expected to be about ninety over the weekend—a record for September. "Perfect weather for fishing," she grumbles.

9:00-9:40 A.M. Jordan spends first-period algebra designing an early birthday card for Sky.

10:13 A.M. Jordan slips the card into Carrie's locker.

11:04 A.M. Carrie seals the card and the fifty dollars in a big red envelope.

12:29 P.M. In the lunch line Carrie asks Sky if she can come over again this afternoon. Sky agrees—as long as Carrie promises not to mention the words Wild World. It's not that she minds missing out. Really. It's just that if she hears those words again, she may scream.

12:31-12:53 P.M. Wild World comes up three times in conversation during lunch.

12:54 P.M. Sky runs to the girls' bathroom and screams at the top of her lungs.

1:37 P.M. Sky slips Alex a note in Ms. Lloyd's English class:

> Carrie is coming over this afternoon. Do you want to come, too?

1:39 P.M. Alex slips Sky the following reply:

> I can't. I'm going skateboarding with Sam. You guys have fun.

2:33 P.M. Alex meets Carrie near the girls' lockers and informs her that the coast will be clear this afternoon—Sky and Carrie will be all alone.

3:15 P.M. Carrie and Sky board the bus. Sky makes Carrie renew her promise not to mention Wild World. Carrie agrees.

Six

For the first time in a long, long while, Sky simply wanted to be by herself. It wasn't as if she was mad at Carrie or anything. She just didn't feel like talking. To anyone.

So she kept her mouth shut as the two of them walked the length of the dock toward the houseboat, wracking her brains for an excuse. At least her parents and Leif weren't around. They were off at a conference at Leif's school. Maybe she could say that she had to scrub the decks or something. It was such a nice day. . . .

"Hey, Sky, are you all right?" Carrie asked suddenly.

Sky shrugged. "Um . . . I actually have a lot of chores to do and stuff," she mumbled, pushing open the door to the main cabin. She flopped down on the brown couch. "Maybe we should just hang out tomorrow or the next day," she added, avoiding Carrie's eyes.

"Okay," Carrie agreed cheerfully.

Sky looked up. That had been easy. She'd actually been expecting a little more resistance. But Carrie was just standing by the open door, with her thumbs hooked under the straps of her backpack, smiling as the breeze rustled her black hair.

"I want to give you something before I go, though," Carrie said. She wiggled out of her backpack and put it on the floor, then squatted down and pulled a big red envelope out of the front pocket. She held it up to Sky casually.

Now Sky was totally confused. "What is that?" she asked.

"Just take it," Carrie said, flapping it a few times in front of Sky's face.

Sky reached forward and took the envelope hesitantly, keeping her eyes pinned on Carrie.

"It's an early birthday present," Carrie said with a big smile.

Sky started shaking her head, but she was grinning. "An early birthday present?" she echoed. She tore the envelope open carefully. "But my birthday isn't until . . ."

Her jaw dropped.

"What the—" she gasped.

There was money in there. Horrified, she gazed at Carrie, then back at the envelope. Her hands were trembling. She pulled out the bills and started counting. Ten, twenty, thirty . . . fifty dollars. Her breath started coming fast. This couldn't be happening. She was holding fifty dollars in her hand—enough to pay for the day at Wild World.

Sky stared at the bills in her fist. Her mind was racing. She could go! She could go to Wild World. Images of roller coasters and junk food and souvenir T-shirts flashed through her mind. But wait—she had told her friends she was busy and they had done this anyway. Why? Sky suddenly felt sick as she realized that Carrie must have somehow discovered the truth.

"Look at the card!" Carrie cried, laughing.

"What is this?" Sky hissed, glaring at her.

Carrie's laughter faded. "What do you mean? I told you, it's a birthday present—"

"I don't want it!" Sky shouted. Rage flashed through her like a jolt of electricity. How could they do this? Did they have to prove to her how easy it was for them to get an extra fifty bucks? She thrust the wad of cash at Carrie. The card and envelope fell to the couch, forgotten. "Take it back!"

The color drained from Carrie's face. She looked as if she had been punched. "Sky, what—what's the matter?" she stammered.

Sky stared at Carrie without seeing her. Had it been that pathetically clear to her friends how much she wanted to go to Wild World? Did they feel sorry for her? Maybe they felt sorry for her all the time.

"I told you, I don't want your lousy money!" Unable to control herself, Sky simply threw the crumbled bills at Carrie. They fluttered to the floor like fallen leaves. "What makes you think I do?"

Carrie swallowed. "I—I . . . we just thought you'd

want to come with us this weekend," she whispered tremulously. "So we all pitched in. I told you, it's a present—"

"Well, I don't accept it," Sky interrupted. "Why do you even think I want to come with you? I told you already—I'm busy."

"I know, but—"

"No buts!" Sky cried.

Carrie shook her head. "Sky, please," she pleaded. "I didn't know it would make you so mad."

Sky pushed herself off the couch and took a few deep breaths, struggling to remain calm.

"Listen," Sky said finally. Her voice was low and even. "I made up that story about fishing with Leif because I didn't want to go on your dumb trip to the lousy amusement park. It has nothing to do with money, all right?"

Carrie was just shaking her head. "Sky, you know that's not true," she murmured.

"How would you know?" Sky demanded. "Look—just get out of here." She bent down and snatched up the money, then stuffed it into Carrie's bag and shoved the bag into Carrie's hands. "I mean it."

For a moment, their eyes locked.

"Sky, you've got it all wrong," Carrie said desperately.

"No, you've got it all wrong," Sky shot back. "So take a hike."

Carrie flinched. "Sky, please—"

"I mean it, Carrie," Sky warned.

Finally, Carrie just nodded. She let out a deep, shaky breath and slung the backpack over her shoulder. Without another word, she left the boat and scurried up the dock toward Pike's Way.

Sky slammed the door behind her. For a moment, she was too tense to even move. She'd never yelled like that at anyone in her life.

Then again, nobody had ever made her feel so incredibly pathetic.

Skyler Foley
Speaks Out Against Pity

I'm sorry—but this whole Wild World thing has gotten way out of control.

After Carrie left, I sort of went a little crazy. (Well, I guess I went a little crazy before she left, too.) I mean, I went through like a billion emotions in the space of about five minutes.

At first I was so excited and, well, I guess, greedy. I'd just been handed the most money I've ever had at one time. I pictured myself at Wild World—with no worries about how much it was costing or how my family would have to sacrifice so I could go and enjoy myself. Then I figured out the reason why I was able to go: My best friends pitied me.

Then I got mad. I'm talking more mad than I've ever been in my entire life.

But then I felt incredibly guilty. I've never been that harsh to anyone, especially one of my best friends. I hate when people argue. I never say things like "Take a hike." I can't believe that was really me screaming. I must have picked up the phone at least ten times to call Carrie to apologize, but I always ended up slamming it back on the hook before I started dialing.

That's when the embarrassment kicked in. I was embarrassed for the way I threw a temper tantrum in front of Carrie. I was embarrassed for the way I told everyone that dumb lie about taking Leif fishing. I was embarrassed for the way they figured it out so easily.

Most of all, I was embarrassed that money mattered so much to me. And then I got mad at my parents for making money so important to me by not caring about it themselves. I imagined everyone handing Carrie ten dollars and saying, "Poor Sky. She's dying to come to Wild World, but her parents are poor. Let's help her out so her life won't be so lame."

And that's when the embarrassment went away and I started to get angry again. The last thing I want from anyone—especially people I care about—is pity. I mean, when I saw what was in that envelope, I literally felt like a dog. I'm serious. I felt like a little puppy who was getting a treat or something. Because it was like Carrie was saying, "Good old Sky. We feel so bad for you. But since you're such a swell girl, we'll give you a free ride."

So what was I supposed to do? There's no way I could ever thank my friends, or repay them, or anything—and she knew it. The only thing I could do was throw the money back at her to try and save a little of my pride.

I've never felt so small in my life.

Seven

"Whoa!" Alex cried, wobbling on her skateboard. The moment she turned onto Yesler Street, she was blinded by a golden-orange flash of late-afternoon sunlight. It was as if the entire sun had fallen to Earth and had landed right on top of Puget Sound.

Luckily, she regained her balance and once again glided effortlessly toward her driveway. She didn't even bother slowing down. She couldn't see a thing, of course—but when it came right down to it, Alex thought she could probably skate all of Taylor Haven blindfolded.

"Mersel looks for the shot," she heard Matt cry. "The ball goes up—"

Mersel? Alex squinted through the light.

Now this was weird. Carrie was playing basketball. With Matt. She was clattering around the Wagners' driveway in her combat boots and long black skirt, hopelessly trying to put the ball through the little hoop above the garage door.

Alex skidded to a stop and flipped the skateboard up into her hands. "Uh—what's going on here? Aren't you supposed to be at Sky's?"

Carrie dropped the ball. "Yeah. *Supposed* to be," she murmured.

Before Alex could ask any more questions, Matt said, "I told her that if she played some hoops, she might feel better." He scooped up the ball, dribbled a few times, then put up a shot that swished through the net. "Wagner wins again!" he cried.

"What happened?" Alex asked nervously.

Carrie shrugged. "Sky told me to take a hike," she said.

Alex just stared at her. That couldn't be right. Sky would never tell Carrie to take a hike. That would be like . . . well, like if Carrie suddenly decided to play basketball in her combat boots.

Uh-oh.

"She did?" Alex asked, swallowing.

"Yup," Carrie said miserably. She shook her head and attempted a weak smile. "You know, Alex, I should have listened to you. You said Sky wasn't gonna go for it. And you were right. You were more than right—"

"So, are you ready to play another game or what?" Matt interrupted, twirling the ball on his fingers.

Alex rolled her eyes. "Matt—will you shut up? This is serious."

"No, it isn't," Matt said, smirking. "You guys always get into these dumb little fights. But instead of discussing your problems like civilized . . ."

"Let's go inside," Alex whispered as she tugged

Carrie's sweater. "I really don't want to hear all the new vocabulary words Matt learned this week."

"Ditto," Carrie muttered.

The two of them turned and headed up the front walk to the house.

"Wait!" Matt yelled. "I'm not finished—"

Alex shut the door behind them. "Hi, Dad! I'm home," she called. She tossed her skateboard into the hall closet.

"Hi, Alex!" he answered from his study. "How was your day?"

"Better ask me later," Alex replied, following Carrie up the stairs and into her bedroom. She stepped across all the dirty laundry, then swept some books off her desk chair and onto the floor so that Carrie could have a place to sit.

"So what happened?" she asked worriedly. "What did Sky do?"

Carrie shrugged, then slouched down into the chair. "There really isn't much to tell. I tried to give Sky the fifty bucks, and she wouldn't take it. She got really offended. I tried to explain that it was a birthday present, but she wouldn't listen."

"She was probably too embarrassed," Alex mumbled. She began pacing around the room.

"But why would she get embarrassed over something so minor?" Carrie wondered out loud.

Alex paused. "It's minor to you," she said quietly. "Not to her."

Carrie gave her a quick glance, then looked at the floor. "I guess you have a point," she muttered. "I'm really worried, Alex. Sky's never been this mad at me before."

"Well, Sky isn't the kind of person who holds a grudge," Alex pointed out. "When did all this happen?"

Carrie sighed. "Right after the bus dropped us off."

"So it's been a couple of hours." Alex took off her cap and began fidgeting with it. "I bet she's calmed down by now. Let's give her a call."

Carrie started shaking her head. "I don't know if that's such a good idea."

"Well, how about if I call her?" Alex suggested.

"Yeah." Carrie anxiously chewed her lip. "Okay. You call her and pretend like you haven't seen me or anything. If she doesn't know I'm here, then maybe she'll tell you why she got so mad at me. . . ." Her voice trailed off.

Jeez. Alex had never seen Carrie this shaken up before. Something pretty serious must have happened this afternoon.

"I'll call her right now," Alex said, hurrying over to the phone by her bed. "Don't worry about it." She picked it up and dialed Sky's number, then glanced back at Carrie, who was now staring dismally at the laces of her combat boots. "I bet she's in a much better—"

"Hello?" Sky answered.

60

"Hey!" Alex took a deep breath, trying to sound as relaxed and normal as possible. "What's up?"

There was a long pause. "If you're calling about the birthday present, Carrie has your share of the money," Sky said flatly.

Wow. Alex gulped. This was worse than she had imagined. "Uh . . . what are you talking about?" she asked hollowly.

"What do you think I'm talking about?" Sky's voice rose. "I don't want your money, and I sure don't want to go to any stupid amusement park with you guys."

"So, I guess, you . . . um, you got the card?" Alex stammered.

"Didn't Carrie tell you?" Sky demanded.

"I haven't talked to her," Alex lied, looking Carrie straight in the eye. "I just got home. What's going on? Why are you so mad?"

"Listen, Alex, I don't want your sympathy or anything," Sky mumbled tiredly. "I didn't ask for any money. All I want is to be—"

"I know you didn't ask for it!" Alex cried. "It was a *gift*. People don't ask for gifts. I didn't ask for that T-shirt you gave me for my birthday, right?"

Sky moaned. "It's different, Alex. That T-shirt didn't cost fifty bucks. Plus, my birthday isn't for another month."

"But money isn't the point," Alex argued.

"Yes it is," Sky said. "It's the *only* point."

Alex opened her mouth, but no words would come. She had no idea how to respond to that. Maybe Sky was right. Maybe money was the only point. She didn't know. She glanced back at Carrie.

"What's going on?" Carrie breathed, staring at her intently.

"Look, just forget about it," Sky mumbled.

Alex shook her head. Holding two conversations at once was way too distracting. "I don't want to forget about it," she murmured, turning away from Carrie and hunching over the phone. "If we made you mad, we're sorry, okay? I mean, can't you see that this is the last thing we wanted to happen?"

Sky sighed loudly. "You guys can be so dumb sometimes. Look, all I want is to be left alone. You all go to this amusement park and have fun, okay? I'll see you tomorrow. Bye."

"Wait—"

There was a sharp *click*.

"Hello?" Alex blinked a few times. Her throat was dry. She tried to swallow but couldn't.

"What's going on?" Carrie whispered.

Alex shook her head. Finally, she placed the phone back on the hook and turned around to face Carrie.

"She . . . uh . . . hung up," Alex said.

Carrie's eyes widened. "She did?"

"Yeah. She also said that we could be really dumb sometimes."

"Oh, brother." Carrie squeezed her eyes closed. "Well, she's right about that."

"No kidding."

For a moment, the two of them sat in silence. Then Carrie opened her eyes. "So what are we gonna do now?"

"Nothing," Alex said resignedly. "I don't think there's anything we can do."

<u>Alex Wagner's Book of Deep Thoughts</u>

<u>Entry 9</u>

Why is it that whenever things seem to be going just great, something terrible happens to mess it all up?

Take last week, for example. Carrie won a fiction contest with one of her stories, and she was going to do a reading at a bookstore in Seattle. She was actually the most excited I've ever seen her. Then The Amys struck with a really vile prank and Carrie got totally freaked out about appearing in public.

And a week before that, Amy Anderson invited me over to her house. I thought I was on my way to being the most hip, girlish, and popular eighth-grader at Robert Lowell Middle School—and then all of a sudden I find out that Amy Anderson is really pure evil disguised as a thirteen-year-old girl with blonde hair and an oversized chest. (Actually, that's how Carrie described her.)

Now this.

I can't even believe it. Why would Sky be so mad? It's totally nuts. I mean, Sky is the one who always says, "It's not that big a deal," or "Don't worry about it," or "Everything's going to be fine." I was sure that once I explained to her that the money was a gift, she would accept our apology. . . .

But she didn't, and none of us know how to deal with it. Carrie and I are completely stumped. Maybe Sam and Jordan will figure out a way to make things better. But Sam hates to butt into other people's business, and Jordan and Sky have probably never had a serious conversation the whole time they've known each other.

At this point, I almost feel like we should just go to wild world without her. I know that sounds harsh—but what other options do we have? Sky says she just wants to be left alone. And if she refuses to let us help her, then it's out of our hands. Maybe she'll learn something. Maybe she'll learn that a gift is just a way of being nice, and that she should learn to accept gifts for what they are. . . .

Or maybe she'll change her mind at the last minute and come with us.

That's what I'm really hoping for.

Eight

Ever since he could remember, Sam Wells had made a conscious effort to stay out of other people's business. At least he tried to. It was kind of hard when your four best friends were also four of the nosiest people in the world.

But Sam's mother had taught him at a very early age that he shouldn't dump all his problems on his friends. Of course, his mother had grown up on a Chinook reservation, where everybody dumped their problems on one guy—an old man whose only purpose in life was to make problems disappear. Whenever something bothered Sam's mom, she had just gone to him. Then, *ta-da!* No more problems. Unfortunately, life off the reservation wasn't quite as simple.

Sam had always thought Robert Lowell Middle School could definitely use a guy like that— somebody with all the answers. The way things stood, nobody had any answers. But that didn't stop people from either sharing their problems or offering advice whenever they had a chance.

That's why Sam couldn't figure out what was

going on with Sky. Normally, she fit the Robert Lowell mold perfectly. She was always sharing her problems, and she was always offering advice, whether people asked her for it or not.

But now, for some reason, she was keeping all of her feelings to herself. It was the first time she'd ever done that. And it was obvious to Sam and the others that it was driving her crazy.

Still, it wasn't until the next morning that Sam finally decided he would break his rule about interfering in another person's business—just this one time. Sky obviously needed somebody to talk to about this whole money thing. She hadn't said a word the entire bus ride. And that was very disturbing. Sky could always be counted on to say something, no matter what kind of a mood she was in.

"Sky, wait up," he called once everyone had filed off the bus and was heading through the big double doors into the school building.

"What's up?" she asked. She was staring dejectedly at the pavement and chomping on a piece of gum.

Sam waited until everyone—including Jordan, Alex, and Carrie—was inside.

"I just wanted to apologize about the birthday card and the money and everything," Sam offered cautiously. "We should have known it would make you mad."

Sky laughed once and looked up. The morning

sunlight glistened in her dark eyes, but her expression remained lifeless. "You know what?" she said. "You're the only one so far who's said that. Everyone else has been like, 'We had no idea it would make you mad.' Carrie and Alex were totally shocked."

"Well . . . that's because they thought they were doing you a favor," Sam said. "When you do somebody a favor, the last thing you want to hear is that the person doesn't even want it."

"So I should feel guilty?" Sky asked slowly.

Sam shook his head. "No. No way." Obviously, that hadn't come out exactly the way he'd wanted it to. "I just meant . . . I can understand why Carrie and Alex were so surprised that you got mad. They really weren't expecting it."

Sky sighed and started chewing her gum again. She tugged at her backpack strap. "So how come you aren't surprised?" she asked after a moment. "You were in on it, too."

Sam shrugged. He grinned slightly in spite of himself. "Well, I was a little surprised. . . ."

Sky started grinning, too.

"Look," he said suddenly. "I just wanted to say that I'm really sorry and I think you should come with us to Wild World. I mean, it would totally bite if you didn't come."

Sky's grin faded. "I can't, Sam. Remember?"

Way to go, he said to himself. So much for making Sky feel better. That had come out horribly, too.

Maybe he just should have stayed out of this. He looked down at his sneakers and scratched his head. "Okay. But I also wanted to say . . . that I, uh . . . see, I understand how you feel."

"Sure you do," Sky said quietly. She glanced at the door. "We're gonna be late for class—"

"No, wait a minute," Sam said. "What I'm trying to say is . . . I know what it's like to keep your problems all bottled up inside you. It's really hard not to share them sometimes." The words tumbled haltingly out of his mouth. He hardly even knew what he was trying to say. "And you're the type of person who needs to talk about your problems—you know, to feel better."

Sky studied his face for what seemed like a long while. Her eyes narrowed. She started blowing a bubble—a big, gooey, pinkish balloon—then abruptly sucked it back in with a loud *pop*.

"Did Carrie and Alex put you up to this?" she asked.

Sam drew his head back, stunned. "No. Why—why would you think that?"

Sky chewed again for a moment. "Because you never talk about personal stuff with anyone," she said simply.

Sam hesitated. He wasn't quite sure how to respond to that. Sky was absolutely right—but he hadn't expected her to be so blunt. "Well, I'm worried about you," he said finally. "I'm worried because you always talk about personal stuff. And for some reason, you aren't now."

The faint beginnings of another grin appeared on Sky's lips. "Well, maybe that's because it's nobody's business," she said.

Sam cocked an eyebrow. "Come on, Sky," he joked. "That doesn't sound like you. You're the world's greatest gossip. Since when has something been nobody's business?"

"Since it's about *me*," she said. She blew another bubble.

Sam swallowed. Maybe he shouldn't have said that, either. He really wasn't very good at this sort of thing. That much was clear.

"You know, I feel like I'm having déjà vu," Sky added. "That's the second time I've heard that in two days."

Sam looked at her. "What, that you're the world's greatest gossip?"

Sky shook her head. "No—that I haven't been sounding like me." She let out a deep breath and rolled her eyes, then laughed. "The lame thing is, I don't even know what 'me' sounds like."

Sam nodded. "I know what you mean," he muttered, mostly to himself.

Sky looked at him questioningly. "You do?"

"Yeah." He shrugged. "I mean . . . sometimes I feel like I sound one way at home and a completely different way here at school."

"Well, everyone feels like that," Sky said. "Nobody talks to their parents the same way they talk to their friends, right?"

Sam shook his head. "No, but it's different. I mean, at home, my mom and my sister Shawna kind of expect me to be one thing . . ." He stopped in midsentence. Sky was staring at him.

"Yeah?" she prodded. "Go on."

Sam smirked. "We're supposed to be talking about you, not me, remember?"

Sky smiled, chewing with her mouth open. "Just finish what you were going to say," she urged.

Sam frowned. How had he gotten himself into this mess? "It's nothing, really," he mumbled. "It's just that . . . see, my mom and Shawna are both still really into all the old Chinook traditions. And I'm not. I'm more like my dad. But sometimes I feel like I have to act a certain way around the two of them just to make them happy."

His face started getting hot. All at once, he felt incredibly uncomfortable. He never talked about this sort of thing. He didn't even know why he had brought it up.

"Believe me, I totally understand what you mean," Sky said reassuringly. "It's like, at my house, my parents expect me to be a happy, peaceful flower child all the time. They don't understand why I get so mad sometimes. They just want me to be mellow like they are."

Sam tried to stifle a laugh, but the sound came out before he could stop it.

"What?" Sky asked.

"Nothing," Sam said. "It's just that I never thought you and I really had all that much in common before."

Sky smiled. "What do you mean? We have tons of stuff in common: Alex, Carrie, Jordan, Robert Lowell—"

"Yeah, but you know . . . aside from what's obvious," Sam said.

"I guess if you really think about it, we do have a lot in common," Sky said matter-of-factly. "I mean, look at it this way: I'm half African-American and you're Chinook. In some ways, we're different from almost everyone else in Taylor Haven, including our best friends."

Sam nodded. "You know, you're right," he said. "I never really—"

Brinnng! The first-period bell sounded, cutting him off.

Sky immediately rushed to the door. "Listen, Sam—I know you're trying to help, but don't worry about me, okay?" she called over her shoulder. "I'm gonna be fine."

The next moment, she was gone.

Sam just stood there.

Man. That conversation had ended way too fast. He felt as if he had just sat down in front of a huge pepperoni pizza, taken one bite, then had it snatched away from him.

But that wasn't even what bothered him most.

What bothered him most was that when Sky had said, "I'm gonna be fine," she had never sounded more unconvincing.

Nine

"Guess what?" Jordan announced to the lunch table, delicately easing himself into a chair as he held a tray full of steaming ravioli. "I figured out a way we can get to Wild World for less than three bucks round-trip—"

He broke off. Nobody was even looking at him. Carrie, Alex, and Sam were all gazing sullenly at their own plates. They weren't even moving. They looked more like defective clothing-store dummies than real human beings.

"All right," he said with a sigh. "What is it *now?*"

"What do you think it is?" Sam asked. "You saw Sky today. She's not only totally bummed out, she's mad at us."

Oops. Jordan gulped. "Oh yeah," he muttered embarrassedly. "That."

As a matter of fact, Jordan hadn't seen Sky since this morning . . . and, well, she hadn't exactly been foremost in his mind. He'd been a lot more concerned with figuring out a cheap way to get to Wild World. But now was probably not the best time to make that confession.

"Where is she?" he asked, glancing around the bustling cafeteria.

"She'll be here soon," Alex said. She poked lazily at her ravioli. "She told me she had to stay after history class today."

He fidgeted with his fork. "So I guess nobody convinced her to accept the money, huh?" he asked quietly.

"Nope," Carrie said. She shook her head. "She doesn't even want to talk to me."

"She'll talk to me—as long as it's not about Wild World," Alex said.

"Even I tried to talk her into going," Sam chimed in miserably. "But I didn't get very far. I got her to smile a couple of times, but that was it."

Suddenly, Jordan noticed that all three of them were staring at him.

His eyes narrowed. "What?" he asked.

"That leaves you, Jordan," Carrie stated. "You're our last hope."

"Last hope for what?" he asked nervously.

"Our last hope for talking Sky into accepting our present, dummy," Sam groaned.

Jordan started laughing. He couldn't help it. He had about as much chance of talking Sky into going to Wild World as he did of learning to love the Robert Lowell lunchtime menu. "Okay . . . let me get this straight," he said. "None of you guys could talk her into coming with us—but you think I can?

Compared to you guys, Sky doesn't even like me all that much."

Carrie shook her head. "Jordan, that's the dumbest thing I ever heard," she said. "Of course she likes you."

Jordan leaned back in his chair and averted his eyes. "Maybe. But I don't think I've ever said anything serious to her before. Usually when we're talking, we're making fun of each other."

"That's why you might have a better chance than the rest of us," Alex said. "If she sees that *you* really want her to go, she'll be . . . touched."

Jordan grinned. "How come I get the feeling that you don't even believe what you're saying?"

"Here she comes!" Carrie suddenly hissed. She jerked her chair back with a short screech and snatched up her tray. Alex and Sam immediately followed.

"What are you doing?" Jordan whispered. He glanced anxiously toward the far set of double doors. Sky was approaching the table slowly, clutching a brown paper bag in her hands.

"Going outside," Carrie said as the three of them scurried from the table. She jerked her head toward the huge glass windows that looked out onto the sun-drenched courtyard. It was crawling with noisy fifth- and sixth-graders. "I want to soak up some sun. Besides, I hate ravioli."

"You guys are gonna get in trouble," Jordan

called after them. "It's only twelve-forty. Seventh-and eighth-graders aren't allowed out until one. If somebody sees you . . ."

His voice faded. He had no idea why he was spouting rules at them. He must have really been desperate. They knew the rules just as well as he did.

"Looks like we've got the table to ourselves today," Sky muttered as she slumped down across from him. "Great."

Jordan watched glumly as Carrie, Sam, and Alex disappeared out the doors. Why did they always end up relying on him to solve their problems?

"How come you're not going with them?" Sky asked, pulling some sort of unidentifiable sandwich from her bag. "You don't want to get in trouble?"

Jordan managed a grin. "Something like that. But also . . . I, uh, wanted to talk to you."

Sky looked up from her sandwich and made a face. "If it's about this weekend, I already told the rest of them, I'm not—"

"Wait, wait, wait," Jordan interrupted, raising his hands. "Well, it's a little bit about that." He cleared his throat. "So, uh . . . let me ask you something. Do you think that Carrie was right to give me the gift certificate that she won for her story?"

Sky took a bite of her sandwich and peered at him closely. She chewed slowly, then swallowed. "What do you mean?"

"I mean . . . do you think I deserved that hundred bucks?"

Sky frowned. "Of course. You kept The Amys away and saved the day."

"So why don't you think that you deserve fifty bucks?" he asked.

"Because I didn't do anything to deserve it," she grumbled, dropping her sandwich on its paper wrapper. "It's totally different."

"How?" Jordan looked her in the eye. "Carrie gave me that certificate as a gift. And the five of us are giving you the money as a gift."

"But I don't want it!" Sky cried. "I didn't do anything!"

Jordan jumped slightly. "All right, all right," he murmured. "I'm sorry . . ."

"Look, can't the two of us just enjoy our lunch in peace?" she asked pleadingly. "I'm sick of talking about this."

Jeez. Jordan nodded. "Okay, I'm sorry—"

"You still don't get why I don't want the money, do you?" she demanded suddenly.

Jordan shrugged. "Not really," he admitted.

"And that's the problem," she said.

Jordan paused, waiting for an explanation. But there was nothing. She was right: He didn't get why she wouldn't accept the money. She had confused him even more. She took another bite of her sandwich.

"So . . . I guess you're not coming?" he asked one last time.

She shook her head. "I guess not."

You want to know what's really, really weird? I always thought that of all my friends, I was the dumbest. Okay—maybe that sounds like I'm being a little harsh on myself. I know I'm not stupid or anything. But I definitely thought that Sam and Jordan and Carrie and Alex were smarter than me.

Until now.

Yup. In the past couple of days, I found out that we're all dumb. As a matter of fact, in some ways, they're a lot dumber than I am.

I mean, why can't they just leave the whole thing alone? Why can't they see that the more they try to convince me to go to Wild World, the worse I feel?

But all they seem to think about are their own feelings. All they think about is how they want to feel good about themselves by giving me fifty bucks. Nobody thinks about how I might feel if I took the money and went to Wild World as their little charity case. They'd all be watching me to make sure I was having a great time because of their "gift." And everything about the whole day would turn into a big reminder of how they have money and I don't.

I almost thought Sam understood this morning. It was like for that one little moment we were closer than we've ever been as friends. What I said to him was true. We do have a lot in common. We both know what it's like to feel different from the people around us. And that means that we both know what it's like to feel really confused sometimes.

But Sam still seems to think that I should accept the "gift," right? So I guess he doesn't actually understand that any better than the rest of them.

What it really comes down to is this: I just want this weekend to be over and done with as soon as possible. Then we can all just get on with our lives and forget about it.

Ten

"Sky!" her father was calling from the main cabin. "Sky, can you come upstairs for a minute?"

What now? Sky wondered dismally. She was sprawled across her narrow bed, gazing at the murky water of the sound as it lapped against the glass of the one porthole in her room. She hadn't really felt like moving since she'd gotten home about a half hour ago. But there wasn't much room to move around her tiny cabin, anyway. Her bed and her desk and her dresser took up nearly all the available space.

"Do I have to?" she called back.

There was a pause. "I can come down there if you like," he replied.

"If you really want to," she answered dully. She swung her legs over the side of the bed and sat up straight, rubbing her eyes.

There was a light knock on the door.

"Come in," she mumbled.

The door opened slightly. Her father's bearded face poked through the crack between the door and the doorjamb. He flashed a big, silly-looking smile.

Sky just stared at him.

"Uh-oh," he said. He pushed the door open the rest of the way. "Now I know something's wrong."

Sky rolled her eyes. "Dad . . ."

"Well, you could at least smile back," he said softly.

Sky shrugged and lay back down on the bed. She stared at the ceiling, mostly because she didn't want to look her father in the eye. "I guess I just don't feel much like smiling right now."

Mr. Foley let out a deep breath, then took a seat at Sky's desk chair. "Want to talk about why?" he asked.

Sky didn't reply. If she kept her mouth shut, maybe he would take the hint that she just wanted to be left alone.

"You're still mad about the trip to the amusement park," he murmured.

"No," Sky lied, rolling over on her side so that her back was turned to him. "I'm just tired, all right?"

He didn't say anything for a few moments. The only sound in the room was the swishing and creaking of the boat rocking gently on the water.

"Where are Alex and Carrie and the rest of them?" he finally asked. "I was expecting to see them today. Usually when it's this nice out, you all love to hang out on the back deck."

"They're at Carrie's," Sky said.

"How come you didn't go with them?" he prodded.

"Because I didn't feel like it, okay?" She rolled over and sat up straight. "Why do you care so much?"

"I care that you're upset," he answered. His deep brown eyes grew serious. "When you're upset, I'm upset."

"Oh, please," she groaned.

"Listen, Sky, we'll both feel better if we talk this through. It's important to talk about—"

"I don't *want* to talk about it!" Sky cried, cutting him off. "Why can't you just act like a normal parent for once and leave me alone?"

Mr. Foley leaned back in the chair and shook his head. "Is that what you think 'normal' parents do?" he asked quietly. "They leave their kids alone?"

Sky flopped back on her bed again. "Look . . . look, just forget it," she said, too frustrated to think of any other response.

"No, Sky, I'm not going to forget it," he said in the same even tone. "This is important."

She squeezed her eyes shut, wishing she could magically beam herself out of her room to someplace far away. Maybe she should have gone to Carrie's house with the rest of them. "Why is it that none of my other friends have to deal with this sort of thing?" she wondered out loud. "Carrie's mom and dad never get involved with her problems."

"I know," Mr. Foley said. "And it's a miracle Carrie has turned out the way she has."

Sky opened her eyes. "What do you mean?"

"I mean that Carrie is growing up to be an extraordinarily sweet and funny and intelligent young lady, all on her own. It seems to me her parents don't even notice. If that's normal, then I'm glad I'm not."

Sky turned back to the porthole. A strange, uncomfortable feeling was enveloping her, and she couldn't quite put her finger on what it was. Maybe it was guilt. Her father didn't know it, but she'd always secretly wished that he were more like Carrie's parents. Even if Mr. and Mrs. Mersel didn't pay as much attention to Carrie as they could have, they always provided for her. That was the important thing. Plus they were sharp and stylish; they always seemed to be going somewhere—each time someplace better than the last.

But Sky's dad was the exact opposite. Her mom, too. They were a lot like this boat, in fact. They just floated in the same old spot—day after day, year after year.

"Doesn't it ever bother you that we're totally different from everyone else?" Sky found herself blurting out in the silence.

"In what way?" Mr. Foley asked.

"In *every* way," Sky moaned. "We live on a boat. You work at home. Mom—"

"Alex's dad works at home," he interrupted calmly. "Right?"

"But Alex's dad makes a lot of money!" Sky yelled.

Mr. Foley didn't say anything.

Uh-oh. Sky glanced at him. Maybe she shouldn't have said that. Her father looked hurt. His eyes were sad, and he was stroking his beard, very slowly and thoughtfully.

"I'm sorry you feel that you don't have enough," he said. His voice was barely a whisper. "We'd all be better off with a little more money. But, Sky . . ." He broke off and shook his head, then took a deep breath. "Sky, we have to be thankful for what we have. We're all healthy, and we have enough to eat. We live in a beautiful neighborhood. But most importantly, we have each other—"

"I know," Sky said. "I'm sorry. I'm sorry." She shook her head. Talking about all this was obviously just as painful for him as it was for her. "I shouldn't have brought it up, okay?"

"Don't be sorry," he said. "Never be sorry for saying what you really think. You should only be sorry for keeping your feelings inside."

Sky managed a smile, which was remarkable—considering the totally tense atmosphere in the room. "Dad, please spare me the hippie stuff," she said softly.

Mr. Foley smiled back. "That's not hippie stuff. That's everyone stuff."

"You're just saying that because you're a hippie,"

she muttered, but her tone was soft.

He laughed once. "Maybe." He stood up. "But, Sky, I want you to know, you can talk about anything with me. Anything at all."

Sky lowered her eyes. "I know," she breathed.

"Good." He sighed and headed for the door. "Well, it's much too beautiful outside to be cooped up in here. I'm going out on the deck. Wanna come?"

"In a minute," she said.

"Okay." He closed the door behind him.

Sky sat perfectly still for several minutes, perched on the edge of her bed. She knew her father was right. She knew she should be thankful—for a lot of things.

But that still didn't make her feel any better about missing out on Wild World.

Eleven

Carrie was too tired to argue anymore.

After sitting with Jordan, Sam, and Alex in her bedroom for almost an hour, she finally gave up. Maybe Alex was right: Maybe they should just go to Wild World without Sky. There was really no other option.

"Are you sure we shouldn't just pick her up on Saturday, anyway?" Jordan asked one last time, peeking through the black velvet curtains at the bright blue sky. "If we just show up at her door, it'll be impossible for her to say no."

Carrie shook her head. She was sitting next to Alex on her bed, with her head propped up against some pillows. "That's the *worst* thing we could do. It would be like kidnapping or something. It would cause a scene. I saw this movie once where—"

"Okay, okay," Jordan said. "We don't need to hear about another movie."

Carrie sighed.

Sam pushed himself off Carrie's floor. He walked over to the window and stood by Jordan, peering longingly outside. "I guess we should go without her. I think we did pretty much all we could. All four of us tried separately to get her to come."

"You know . . . Matt still hasn't tried," Alex murmured. "It might be worth a shot to get him to talk to her."

Carrie shook her head again. "If she didn't listen to us, I doubt she'll listen to Matt." She sighed. "We should just go and enjoy ourselves, then forget about it."

Sam turned around and glanced at Carrie anxiously. "You really think Sky will be able to forgive us if we do that?"

Carrie shrugged. The truth was she didn't think Sky would forgive them for it. But they'd gone too far now, especially with all the talking and planning and bugging Sky to take the fifty bucks. There was no way they could turn back and pretend as if nothing had happened. It was too late.

"We'll just have to wait and see," Alex said, pushing herself off the bed. "Now, I don't know about you guys, but I kind of want to go outside."

"Me too," Jordan and Sam said at exactly the same time.

"So it's all settled, then?" Carrie asked.

The three of them were already scurrying for the door. They didn't even bother to reply—and that was answer enough.

Sam paused in the doorway. "Hey, Carrie, can you show me that Wild World web site?" he asked.

Carrie laughed. "You gotta be kidding me. I have no idea how to turn my parents' computer on."

"I can figure it out," Sam said eagerly. "The computer's in the living room, right?"

Carrie hesitated. Her mom was due home any second. If she walked in and saw one of Carrie's friends at the computer, she might start wondering why Carrie wasn't at the computer, too.

"You feel funny about letting me use it if your mom's not around?" he asked.

Carrie nodded. "Something like that," she said apologetically. Luckily Sam wasn't pushy—unlike Jordan. If Jordan wanted to use her computer, he would just bug her about it until Carrie had to give in. "Can't you look it up at home?" she asked.

Sam shook his head. "My dad's computer is in the shop."

Suddenly, a thought occurred to her. She had a perfectly good, brand-new, unused laptop computer sitting in her closet. Her mom had given it to her last week. Carrie hopped off the bed. "I think I have the answer," she said, hurrying over to her closet.

"Are you coming, Sam?" Alex called from downstairs.

"He'll be down in a second," Carrie answered. "He'll meet you outside."

"Uh . . . what's going on?" Sam asked tentatively.

Carrie opened the closet door, fumbled through a pile of clothes on the floor, then yanked a briefcase-sized black carrying case out of the darkness. "Here you go," she grunted, thrusting the case toward him. The computer was actually pretty heavy—heavier than she remembered. "It's yours."

Sam's eyes bulged. "Is that a . . . ?"

"A computer," she finished for him. She placed it gently on her bed, smiling. "Like I said, it's yours."

He shook his head. "I don't get it," he said, glancing confusedly between Carrie and the black case. "You're lending me your computer?"

She shook her head. "I'm giving you my computer."

His black eyes narrowed, but he was grinning. "Uh . . . wait—wait a sec," he stammered. "Are you sure you know what you're doing?"

Carrie laughed. "Of course I know what I'm doing. *You* need a computer and I don't. I hate computers. So it doesn't make any sense for me to have this."

He ran a hand through his short black hair. "But won't your mom freak out if she knows you gave me your computer?" he asked, staring at Carrie as if she were totally insane.

"Not if she doesn't find out," Carrie said, raising her eyebrows conspiratorially.

Sam took a few steps back. "I don't know . . . ," he mumbled.

"Come on," she urged. "It's just gonna go to somebody else if you don't take it."

He started laughing. "Carrie—this isn't like giving Jordan the gift certificate or Sky the money to go to Wild World. It's totally different."

Carrie raised her hands. "How?"

He jerked a finger toward it. "Because judging from the case alone, I'd say that computer is probably worth more than two thousand bucks."

"The money doesn't matter," she groaned, rolling her eyes. Why did everyone always make such a big deal about money? She felt as if she were talking to Sky all over again. "Look—if it'll make you feel any better, we can just say I'm lending it to you, all right?"

He still looked doubtful. "Well . . ."

"And you can return it anytime you like," Carrie added.

Sam laughed again. "Really, Carrie—"

"Just *take* it, all right!" Carrie laughed along with him.

"Okay, okay." Sam leaned over the bed and carefully lifted the case with both hands—as if he really didn't quite believe he was actually holding it. His black eyes were glazed. "I don't even know how to say thank you," he murmured.

"You just did," Carrie said, smirking.

"And I promise I'll give it back the second you give me the word," he stated breathlessly.

Carrie patted him lightly on the back. "I know, Sam."

"You know what?" he said, finally tearing his

gaze away from it. "I think I'm gonna go home and plug it in right now."

Carrie smiled again. "Good idea."

The next moment, Sam was dashing out the door and down the stairs. "Thanks again, Carrie!" he called.

"No problem!" she yelled back.

The front door slammed.

Carrie shook her head. Well, that had been easy enough. It was weird. For some reason, she suddenly felt better than she had all week. It was as if a load had been lifted from her shoulders. Why were gifts so hard for people to accept? Maybe if she'd just pushed a little harder with Sky . . .

But, no. Sky would never have accepted the money. And in that instant, Carrie realized something. Part of the reason she felt so bad about Sky was that deep down, she was a little hurt. Suddenly it was obvious: Giving presents was just as good as getting them. As far as Carrie was concerned, it was a lot better.

And Sky hadn't allowed Carrie to give. She hadn't allowed *any* of them to give. No wonder they were all so confused and depressed. When Sky refused to take their gift, she had hurt their feelings. She hadn't meant to hurt them, of course— but then again, they hadn't meant to hurt her feelings, either.

But how could Carrie explain that to Sky?

She glanced at the old black typewriter, sitting there on her battered oak desk. The blank page was still sticking out of it, untouched. Maybe they did have one last shot at convincing Sky to go. It was always easier to write something than to actually say it. So if Carrie just sat down and carefully typed out exactly what she was feeling, maybe Sky would understand why they all wanted her to take the money so badly.

It wasn't because they pitied her. It was just that they wanted to give her something. It was that simple. And if anyone could relate to that, it would be Sky, right?

Without another second's hesitation, Carrie sat down at her desk and began pounding away at the keyboard.

Dear Sky,

I know you're probably sick and tired of hearing about Wild World, but I just wanted to say one last time that I'm really sorry if we offended you by trying to give you money. You probably thought that it was because we felt sorry for you. It wasn't. Honestly.

Anyway, what I'm really trying to say is that we just want you to come because we would have a lousy time without you. Plus, if those rides really do make you sick, it would be fun to see you blow chunks all over the place. Just kidding.

But seriously, there's another reason, too.

It's the most important reason. And that's just that it's nice to give somebody a present every once in a while. There's no explanation for that, really. It just feels good.

So when you got so mad at us, we couldn't help but feel bad. We didn't think that it would be such a big deal. It was kind of like what happened when Alex told me not to be so mad at Jordan for handing in my story. She didn't think it was such a big deal, and I did. Later, I found out that she was right.

Hopefully, you'll see things our way and change your mind, too. If you do, you'll be doing us all a big favor. I know that sounds crazy, but it's true. You'll make us feel a lot better. And I know that making us feel better is probably the last thing on your mind right now, but just think about it. Does this make any kind of sense?

Come find me after you get this note—
                    Carrie

mush herself between Carrie and Jordan in that backseat and listen to any more apologies about Wild World.

"Come *on*, Sky," her mom called impatiently, waving her toward the door.

Maybe I'll just sit by myself today, Sky said to herself.

She could always sit next to Joanna Morgan—that weird girl with pigtails and braces who always sat right behind Mel and Aimee. And if Carrie and Alex and Jordan and Sam made a big deal about it, she could just say that it was too hot for all of them to be cramped in the backseat. In a way, that was true.

Yup. Her mind was made up. For once in her life, she was going to do something separate from the group. She would have to get used to being on her own, anyway. It was good training for this weekend. She would sit next to Joanna.

"Have a good day at school, sweetie," her mom said as she lumbered on board.

"I will," she stated.

Brick closed the door behind her. Sky smiled at him sympathetically. The poor guy's ratty old T-shirt was soaked. Even behind his sunglasses, she could see bags under his eyes. Most of his long black hair had fallen out of his ponytail. He looked as if he were about to pass out.

"Sorry to make you wait," she said.

"No problem," he croaked. "It was nice to have

the door open for so long. I'm starting to feel like a microwaved hot dog in here."

"I know what you mean," she muttered. There was no denying it: The air inside the bus was even more heinous than the air outside. It was like a stuffy locker room. She carefully kept her eyes pinned to the floor to avoid looking at the backseat, then slipped in beside Joanna Morgan.

The bus roared down Pike's Way. Wind rushed through the open windows. At least that provided some relief from the heat.

Sky leaned over and began putting on her sandals. She could feel Joanna's curious eyes on her, watching her every move. *Please don't say anything,* Sky begged silently. *Please don't ask why I'm sitting—*

"How come you're not sitting with your friends?" Joanna asked. She had a slight lisp. "Sitting" sounded almost like "thitting."

Sky finished putting on her sandals and shrugged. She should have known Joanna would ask. Everyone at Robert Lowell knew who sat where—and any little change made people wonder and gossip. Including Sky. "It's too hot to be scrunched up back there," she replied as casually as she could.

"Oh," Joanna said. She turned back toward the window.

Sky leaned back in her seat and closed her eyes. Well, at least Joanna had left it at that. Sitting up here wasn't so bad, after all.

The only drawback, of course, was that she was right behind The Amys. She could hear them whispering, as usual.

" . . . yeah, but Jordan . . ."

Sky's hearing perked up. Did they just mention Jordan's name? She kept her eyes closed, but she strained her ears, carefully listening for any other scrap of conversation.

" . . . always at the same table. It's gotta be before lunch."

Sky held her breath. It was difficult to hear over the wind and the bus's motor.

"Did you get the stuff?"

"It's all ready. It'll never come out."

". . . excellent that he's got blond hair."

Sky couldn't even tell who was speaking. She couldn't even tell what they were talking about—but whatever it was, it was bad. That much was totally obvious.

"No, not before. We got Carrie before lunch. It's gotta be after. Jordan is always the last one to leave. . . ."

". . . aim has to be perfect."

"Oh, I won't miss, believe me. . . ."

The roar of the motor grew louder. Sky lost the rest of the conversation.

But she'd heard all she needed to hear.

The Amys were going to get Jordan today.

Why not? It made total sense. Almost a week had passed since Jordan's prank. His guard would be

99

down. They would be getting him when he least expected it.

Sky's eyelids opened. She let out a deep breath. Amy Anderson was still leaning over the back of her seat, huddled closely with Mel and Aimee. They obviously hadn't noticed that she had been listening. Sky couldn't help but get majorly depressed as she watched them. The Amys could even make *scheming* look glamorous. They were all wearing incredibly fashionable floral summer dresses—the kind you only saw in catalogs but you could never afford. They were all made up. They almost looked like triplets.

Sky turned and stared past Joanna's pigtails at the passing evergreens, nervously twirling some hair around her finger. What were they going to do? They definitely weren't going to be content to spray Jordan with a water gun, like they had sprayed Carrie. No, they were going to do something much, much worse.

But what?

Before she could even make a guess, the bus turned onto the semicircular drive in front of the school and jerked to a stop. The Amys broke up their huddle. As Amy turned around in her seat, Sky could see her wicked smile under a flash of long blonde hair.

Yup—they were planning something bad. Worse than bad. Totally crushing.

Sky knew right then: *I have to warn Jordan.*

No matter how angry she was at him, he didn't deserve this. The Amys were going to humiliate him. Nobody deserved to be humiliated like that. Especially someone—like Jordan—who had done so much for his friends. He'd singlehandedly taken on The Amys just so the rest of them could enjoy Carrie's reading.

It was time for Sky to return the favor. For today anyway, she needed to forget the money thing and put her hang-ups aside. And that's what she was going to do.

Thirteen

"I still can't believe she didn't sit with us this morning," Jordan muttered as he and Sam jostled their way through the crowded hall toward their first-period social studies class. "Sky *lives* for the backseat. She's never sat anywhere else."

Sam nodded grimly. "I told you, man—she's really mad."

Jordan sighed. "I think Sky is overreacting, don't you?"

"Maybe," Sam said, shrugging. "It depends on your point of view."

Jordan stopped in his tracks. "Hold on. So you're saying that trying to give a gift to someone you care about is—"

"*Pssst!*"

Jordan glanced over his shoulder. Was somebody talking to him?

"Jordan!" a girl's voice hissed. "Over here!"

Suddenly Jordan saw Sky. She was standing about ten feet away from him on the stairs that led to the second floor—waving frantically. He couldn't believe it. Sky had ignored all four of them on the bus, but now she was in the mood to talk?

"Come *on*," she urged.

Jordan looked at Sam, totally bewildered.

The first-period bell rang.

"I gotta go to class, man," Sam said, backing away. "You're on your own." He disappeared into the crowd.

"Thanks," Jordan mumbled. He should have known that Sam wouldn't want to hang around. Somehow he had a feeling that Sky didn't want to make pleasant chitchat. He sighed, then pushed his way through the dwindling crowd toward the stairs where Sky was waiting for him.

"Come closer," Sky whispered. She brushed some of her curly brown hair behind her ear and leaned over, glancing a couple more times up and down the deserted hall. Jordan couldn't help but notice how nervous she looked. She had a weird expression on her face—like she had just broken every major school rule or something.

"What's up?" Jordan asked hesitantly.

She cupped her hands over her mouth and bent close to Jordan. "You have to skip lunch today," she breathed into his ear. "The Amys are planning to get you."

Jordan's eyes widened. He'd been expecting to hear a lot of things, but not that. His head jerked up. "What?" he shrieked. "Are you sure? How did you find out?"

"Shh," Sky whispered. She held a finger over her mouth and peeked back down the hall. "I'm telling you—I'm sure," she murmured hurriedly. "I don't know what it is, but I know it's gonna happen in the cafeteria today."

Jordan stared at her. He was starting to feel vaguely ill.

"I overheard them on the bus this morning," Sky whispered, and the scared expression on her face was enough to convince him that she was telling the truth. "Look—I can't be late for class." She started scrambling up the second flight of stairs. "Just promise me you won't go to lunch!" she hissed.

"Well—well, where should I go?" he stammered desperately.

"Try the infirmary," she muttered over her shoulder. "It always works for me."

The infirmary? That wouldn't work for him. He had a bad track record with Nurse Simmons. For some reason, she never believed him, even if he was sick. He opened his mouth again—but Sky had already rounded the corner and bolted up to the second floor.

For a couple of long moments, he just stood there on the staircase.

Then he swallowed.

Whoa. Jordan had known deep down The Amys would get him sooner or later, but somehow knowing exactly when and where made it scarier. It was like knowing the time you were going to be strapped into the electric chair or something.

So what could he do?

Well, at least he had been warned. That was the good thing. The bad thing, of course, was that The Amys would get him sooner or later anyway. If they messed up this time, they would be extra certain not to mess up the next time. The other bad thing was that he would definitely have to miss lunch today, and he'd be starving by the time school was over.

But that was the Law of Jordan Sullivan. Two bad things for every good one.

"Shouldn't you be somewhere, Mr. Sullivan?" a deep voice asked.

Jordan whirled around.

Principal Cashen was standing in the hall. He looked mad. His shirtsleeves were rolled up and his tie was loose—and his bald head was glistening with sweat. Obviously, the heat wasn't doing much for his mood.

"Uh, yeah," Jordan mumbled, scurrying down the stairs. "I'm just running a little late this morning. Sorry."

"I'm sure you are," Principal Cashen mused. "You can think about how sorry you are this afternoon when you're sitting in detention. For one hour."

Jordan hesitated, cringing slightly. "You want me to . . . ?" He let the sentence hang.

"That's right," Principal Cashen stated. "This isn't

the first time you've been late for class, Mr. Sullivan. I can't tolerate excessive tardiness. Now run along before I give you two hours' detention."

Perfect, Jordan thought. So on top of everything, he was going to have to stay late on a Friday afternoon.

But then, all of a sudden, a crazed idea flashed through his brain.

"Hey, Principal Cashen?" he asked. "I just remembered. I have a doctor's appointment this afternoon, so—"

"Don't try it, Mr. Sullivan," the principal said coldly. "That trick doesn't even work with *fifth*-graders."

"No, really, I'm not trying to get out of detention," Jordan insisted. "Can I just do it during lunch?"

Principal Cashen's eyes narrowed. "You're willing to give up your lunch hour to sit in detention?" he asked, smiling dubiously. "Do you enjoy sitting in stifling hot classrooms?"

"No, but I *really* have a doctor's appointment," Jordan lied.

"Well . . ." Finally, the principal nodded. "Okay. Be in my office no later than twelve-fifty. It would be cruel to have you do the whole hour at once on such a hot day. You can do the other half on Monday."

"Thanks!" Jordan cried. He turned and sprinted down the hall toward his social studies class.

"I mean it, Mr. Sullivan," Principal Cashen called after him. "Not a second past twelve-fifty."

"I'll be there," Jordan answered as his footsteps pounded on the floor. "Don't worry. You can count on it."

Friday:

What are friends for, anyway . . . ?

8:48 A.M. Sky rushes off the bus before anyone can talk to her. Her mind is racing. She's got to warn Jordan.

8:56 A.M. Sky warns Jordan of The Amys' plan and dashes off to her first-period class.

8:58 A.M. Amy Anderson bumps into Sky in the hall outside of Mr. Engel's first-period math class. She apologizes, then hurries off. Sky panics that Amy saw her talking to Jordan.

9:04 A.M. Mr. Engel removes a sign taped to the back of Sky's T-shirt. The sign reads: "Don't hate me because I'm a dork."

10:15 A.M. Sky finds a typed note in her locker. She feels sick. Carrie has finally gone off the deep end. Does she really expect Sky to take the money now—because *Carrie's* feelings are hurt?

10:17 A.M. Sky runs to the girls' bathroom and screams.

Her friends are such jerks. She should have just let Jordan get tortured by The Amys.

11:35 A.M. Sky accidentally meets Carrie in the hall near their lockers. She tells Carrie that if Carrie wants to feel good about giving money away, she should donate it to a charity, not to her. Before Carrie can reply, Sky storms off.

12:31 P.M. Sky can't face sitting with everyone in the cafeteria. She decides to eat lunch in the courtyard. Besides, she's done her duty. Jordan's been warned.

12:35 P.M. Sky takes her sandwich out of the bag. She glances through the huge windows into the cafeteria. She gasps, drops her sandwich, and rushes back into the school.

Fourteen

I

Carrie was the first to arrive at the lunch table that Friday—and she didn't know what to expect.

She was pretty sure Sky would find an excuse to avoid lunch again. And Carrie was actually starting to get a little irritated.

It hadn't been easy to write what she had written. She wasn't the most touchy-feely person in the world or anything, and Sky knew that. But Sky had still been completely rude, which made Carrie feel even worse than before.

As a matter of fact, if Sky did show up for lunch today, maybe Carrie would just give her a piece of her mind. She would tell Sky—very calmly, of course—that Sky wouldn't have to worry about any more unexpected gifts from her friends. Because she wouldn't be getting any. Nope. No way. Never again. Carrie had learned her lesson, and she was sure the others would agree. No more gifts for Sky.

Then Carrie thought about how sad Sky had looked this past week, and she put her head in her hands. Maybe she wouldn't say anything at all.

II

Jordan stood at the end of the slow-moving lunch line, glancing anxiously around the cafeteria. Carrie was the only one at the table. Nobody else had arrived. But Amy, Mel, and Aimee were all daintily eating gray mystery meat at their table, just waiting for him.

Jordan swallowed. Where *was* everyone? It was already twelve thirty-five. He had purposely waited by his locker a few extra minutes in hopes that he would be the last of the group to arrive—just in case The Amys changed their plan and tried to get him before lunch.

He rubbed a sweaty palm through his tangled blond hair, peering at The Amys out of the corner of his eye. Was it his imagination, or was it a million degrees in the cafeteria? Maybe The Amys were planning on bombarding him with water balloons. That wouldn't be so bad. It would be kind of nice to cool off. . . .

There was a tap on his shoulder.

"Ah!" His heart lurched. He spun around, nearly dropping his tray.

Alex and Sam were standing behind him, holding their skateboards.

"Don't sneak up on me like that!" he gasped, wide-eyed.

Alex and Sam looked at each other.

"Uh . . . sorry," Alex said, grinning slightly.

"Didn't mean to scare you. Although the lunch line is kind of spooky."

Jordan just shook his head. Now was not the time for sarcasm. His breath was coming fast. His pulse was racing.

Sam's brow grew furrowed. "Are you all right, man?" he asked carefully. "You look a little edgy."

"I *am* a little edgy," he hissed. He jerked his head once toward The Amys' table. "The Amys are gonna get me today—*here*."

Sam and Alex exchanged another confused glance.

"How do you know?" Alex whispered.

"Sky told me," he whispered back. "She overheard them on the bus this morning."

Their mouths fell open at the same time.

"I'll explain everything later," he muttered. "Just stick by me, all right? This might get ugly."

Sam started shaking his head. "But—"

"I mean it," Jordan warned. He slid his lunch tray onto the counter, then grabbed a plate of steaming mystery meat and white mush—which was probably supposed to pass for meatloaf and mashed potatoes. His stomach squeezed into a tight knot. He had absolutely no appetite. But that was okay. If worse came to worst and The Amys did try something, the stuff on his plate would be perfect for a food fight.

III

Sky pushed open the big double doors that led to the cafeteria and stared in amazement.

She had seen what she'd thought she'd seen: Jordan *was* here.

He was at the lunch counter with Alex and Sam, staring right at The Amys. She couldn't believe it. He might as well have been wearing a sign that said: "Get me."

Sky shook her head. What was he thinking? She'd told him specifically not to come to lunch. In plain English. If there was ever a time that he earned the nickname Jor-*dumb*, it was right now.

Yup, he had really messed up this time. Sky decided she would just have to take matters into her own hands and try to save Jordan. And there was only one solution. Somehow she had to distract The Amys long enough for Jordan to wolf down his lunch and get his behind out of there.

Without hesitating another moment, Sky marched through the cafeteria, sat herself down at the one empty seat at The Amys' table, smiled casually, and said, "Mind if I join you guys?"

All three of The Amys held their forks in midair and just gaped at her.

Sky pulled some carrot sticks out of her bag and began eating. Then she looked up at them. "I'm not bothering you guys, am I?" she asked, trying to sound as friendly as she could possibly manage.

Amy Anderson's lips pressed into a tight line. Her bright blue eyes were slits. "What are you trying to pull, Sky?" she growled. "You think this is funny? It's too hot for stupid games."

Sky finished her mouthful and dabbed her moist forehead with a napkin. "What?" she asked blankly, blinking a few times.

"Get out of here," Aimee whispered, thrusting a finger in Carrie's direction. "Go sit with your loser friends."

Sky shook her head. "I'm tired of sitting with my loser friends." She flashed a wide grin at Amy. "See, when you stuck that note to my back this morning, it got me thinking. You were right. I *am* a dork. So I figured if I sat with you guys, I wouldn't be a dork anymore because—"

"Shut up," Aimee hissed. "Will you just shut up and get out of here?"

Sky shrugged and popped another carrot in her mouth. Hopefully none of them could see how nervous and miserable she really was.

Amy pushed her tray aside and leaned across the table, fixing Sky with an icy glare. "Sky, I don't want to be rude. But we don't want you to sit with us. So what can we possibly do to make you leave?"

Sky returned her gaze. "Nothing," she said evenly. "Nothing at all."

IV

Carrie was still in a state of frozen, horrified shock when Alex, Sam, and Jordan joined her.

"Ca-Can you *believe* this?" she spluttered, unable to tear her eyes from Sky. "She's lost it. She's totally lost it. Somebody needs to lock her up in an insane asylum before she hurts herself."

"No—somebody needs to give her a medal," Jordan muttered.

Carrie swiveled around in her chair. "*What?*" she demanded.

"She's only sitting there to distract them," Jordan said under his breath. "They're looking to get revenge for what I did last Sunday—right here and now."

Carrie leaned back in her chair. It took her a few moments to process what Jordan had just said. Sky was sitting with The Amys to distract them? She glanced at Alex and Sam.

"It's true," Alex whispered. "Sky overheard them talking about it on the bus this morning. They want to get Jordan at lunch today."

In spite of all her confusion, a strange tingle was creeping up the base of Carrie's spine. Was this for real?

"What are they going to do?" she murmured anxiously.

Jordan lifted his shoulders. "Sky doesn't know," he said.

Carrie frowned. "But—"

"You know what?" Jordan interrupted. "I thought I was hungry, but I'm not. I think I'm gonna split. I have to get to detention, anyway. Would you guys mind taking my tray up for me?"

Carrie started shaking her head. *Detention?* "Whoa, slow down here," she said. "You gotta explain what's going on. . . ."

But Jordan was already standing up. For a brief instant, his eyes locked with Amy Anderson's. Then he turned and made a beeline for the exit. The double doors slammed behind him.

Carrie turned to Alex. "Will you *please* tell me what's going on here?" she demanded.

"We told you all we know," Alex said, slouching back in her chair. She took her Sonics cap off and started fanning her face with it. "Sky is sitting there to protect Jordan. It's true."

Carrie glanced back at The Amys' table one last time. All three of The Amys were now glowering at Sky.

Sky calmly finished the last carrot stick, crumpled her bag in her hands, then stood.

"Hey!" Amy Anderson yelled. She reached for the backpack that was tucked under her chair. Carrie held her breath. From past experience, she knew there was probably a water gun in there—or something worse.

Get out of there, Sky, Carrie commanded silently.

Sky dashed out the other set of doors just as Amy

reached into her backpack. Carrie stood up and stared hard, trying to get a better view of what was inside. Luckily, by that time, Carrie wasn't the only one staring at Amy. Almost everybody else in the lunchroom was, too.

Amy froze. "What are you all looking at?" she demanded angrily, zipping up her backpack and sliding it under her chair. She picked up her fork again.

Slowly, they all went back to their lunches. Everyone except Carrie. She was still too stunned to move. Everything had happened so fast.

"Sky really was sitting there to distract them," she murmured to herself in disbelief.

"Of course she was," Sam said. "Why else would she sit there?"

All at once, Carrie felt incredibly ashamed. She had actually been planning to yell at Sky when she saw her.

But in spite of everything—in spite of the note, in spite of the fact that she was angry at all of them— Sky had still been willing to sacrifice herself for her friends. In typical Sky fashion, she'd thought of someone else before she thought of herself.

"Wow," Carrie said finally.

"I think Jordan was right," Sam said. "I think Sky does deserve a medal."

"Well, we can't give her a medal," Alex mumbled. "She probably wouldn't accept it."

Carrie nodded as she flopped into her chair.

"You're right," she said firmly. She looked at the two of them. "So we just have to figure out something she will accept."

Fifteen

Sky didn't know why she had bothered to put on her bathing suit. She didn't feel like swimming at all. But her mom and dad and Leif had bugged her all morning to come swimming with them—until finally she had just put on her suit to shut them up.

Now the three of them were in the water, splashing around in total bliss. It was enough to make her scream. To make matters worse, the temperature today was supposed to be even hotter than the day before. It was supposed to get up to around ninety-four. It already felt like ninety-four inside the main cabin of the boat. Sky's normally bouncy hair hung limply around her face, and her lime green one-piece suit literally felt as if it were glued to her body.

"Sky!" Lief shrieked from the water, laughing with delight. "Sky—we're gonna play Marco Polo! Come on!"

Sky slumped back in the brown couch. *Awesome,* she grumbled inwardly. Alex and Carrie were probably careening down a jumbo water slide at this very moment—and she was being invited to play some boring game with her boring family in the stagnant green water outside her own boring house. Maybe Amy Anderson had been right, after all. Maybe she was a dork.

"Sky?" Mrs. Foley called. "You should really come in. The water feels great."

"In a minute," she called back. She knew deep down that they were all just trying to make her feel better, but knowing that didn't help much. It didn't help at all, in fact. Today was going to be a long and totally lame day. And there was nothing she could do about it.

Sighing, she pushed herself off the couch. She might as well cool off, at least. . . .

She froze.

A black Mercedes was slowing to a stop on Pike's Way, right at the end of the dock. A very familiar black Mercedes. Sky squinted through the window. The car looked exactly like the one that belonged to Carrie's mom . . .

"No!" she gasped out loud.

It was the Mersels' car. Carrie and Jordan and Sam were getting out the back door. They were all dressed in their amusement park clothes: sunglasses and long T-shirts over swimsuits and sandals. Sky watched helplessly as they ran around to the trunk and started taking all kinds of stuff out of the car: a cooler, a boom box, towels . . .

This can't be happening, she said to herself. Had

they decided to take her to Wild World anyway? Even after everything she'd said to them?

Why else would they be here with all their gear? Mrs. Mersel was probably footing the entire bill herself. After all that had happened, her friends still hadn't taken no for an answer. They were still determined to destroy her pride in order to make themselves feel generous.

Carrie finished unloading the car and slammed the trunk shut. The Mercedes zoomed off in the direction of Ocean's View. The three of them gathered up all of the belongings and started heading toward the boat.

Sky shook her head. She was totally confused now. What were they doing? She burst out the front door and stormed down the length of the dock to face them.

"What's going on?" she demanded.

Carrie was struggling with the cooler. "Hey—can you give me a hand with this?" she grunted. "It's really kind of heavy."

"Are you nuts?" Sky yelled.

Carrie let the cooler fall to the dock with a loud *thud*, rattling some ice and cans.

"Uh-oh," Carrie said, wiping the sweat off her pale forehead with her arm. Her expression remained blank under her black shades. "I shouldn't have done that. I think some of those Cokes are going to explode—"

"Good!" Sky snapped. What was Carrie trying to prove? Sky hadn't even talked to Carrie since yelling at her about the note. Now Carrie was standing on her dock, complaining about exploding Cokes as if nothing had happened. The whole thing was absolutely, totally insane.

Sam and Jordan were also trying to make their way to the boat—Sam with an armful of towels and Jordan with the boom box—but Sky planted her feet firmly in the middle of the dock so they couldn't pass.

"Will you please tell me what you're doing?" she asked, folding her arms across her chest. "I told you, I don't want to go on your stupid trip—"

"Shh," Jordan interrupted. "I think I hear something."

Sky's face grew flushed. This was ridiculous. "I will not shush! You guys—"

"Yeah," Sam cut in dryly. "I hear it, too. I can't believe they're here already. That was fast."

Sky opened her mouth again to yell at Sam—then hesitated. She actually heard something, too: the unmistakable rumble of an approaching motorboat. Her eyes narrowed. "What is going on here? Who's coming?"

Jordan and Sam both looked back at Carrie.

"I called Wild World, and they said the wait to get in was gonna be at least two hours," Carrie said, shrugging. "I guess everybody in the state of

Washington had the same idea that we did. Anyway, it's way too hot to stand in lines all day, so I called Alex, and she convinced Matt to take us waterskiing. Now will you please help me with this cooler? I'm dying to get into the water."

Sky blinked. Suddenly, she forgot her anger. It seemed to melt away, like ice in the cooler under the hot sun.

"Waterskiing?" she murmured.

"That's right," Carrie said. The faintest hint of a smile passed across her lips.

"Matt said it was perfect weather for it," Jordan added, shifting the boom box from one hand to the other. "He had already planned on bagging the whole Wild World trip anyway, even before he found out there was a wait. The water's like glass. Perfect waterskiing conditions."

Sky swallowed. She loved waterskiing. Aside from shopping, waterskiing was pretty much her favorite activity in the world.

And everyone knew it.

Now . . . this couldn't have been a coincidence, could it?

Just then, the Wagners' little speedboat rounded the bend. Matt was at the wheel, and Alex was right beside him, bundled up in a bright-orange life jacket and holding extras. The boat was loaded with several pairs of skis.

Sky watched slack-jawed as the engine quieted to

a whisper and Matt carefully steered the boat up alongside the dock.

"What's going on?" Mr. Foley called, treading water and poking his head out from behind the houseboat.

"We're going waterskiing," Matt called back, running a hand through his windswept brown curls. He glanced up at Sky with a wry grin. "If that's okay with you," he said.

"Uh . . . uh . . ." Sky stammered, unable to say anything else.

"She means yes," Alex called back.

"Great!" Mr. Foley exclaimed. "Have fun, Sky!"

Sky turned to Carrie again. The faint hint of a smile that had been on Carrie's face a minute ago was now a full-fledged grin.

"Is there really a wait at Wild World?" Sky asked suspiciously.

"Of course there is," Carrie replied, peering over her sunglasses. "Now, for the third and last time—will you help me with this stupid cooler?"

Sky started laughing. She couldn't help it. "As long as you're telling the truth," she said.

Carrie sighed. "Of course I'm telling the truth. Now let's get going before we all get broiled to death."

Sky looked at her. Just as Carrie pushed her glasses back up the bridge of her nose, Sky caught a glimpse of her hazel eyes. They had a sort of devilish glint to them—but they were also soft at the same time . . . almost apologetic. And at that moment, Sky understood perfectly what Carrie had been trying to say in her note. It was nice to give.

But every once in a while, it was also nice to accept.

Sky smiled. "So let's get going," she said.

Skyler Foley's
Final Confession

I feel sort of bad. After having a totally awesome time skiing, I never got to apologize to Carrie for yelling at her about the note. Of course, she never apologized, either. So there's this kind of unspoken forgiveness between us.

But that's fine. In a way, that's one of the nicest things about my friendship with Carrie. A lot of times, we don't have to say anything at all. We each know what the other is thinking.

That's the best thing about my friendship with all of them, as a matter of fact. Even though I knew why they decided to go waterskiing instead of going to Wild World, nobody mentioned it. Well, actually, Jordan thanked me a couple of times for saving him from The Amys on Friday. The waterskiing trip probably had a little something to do with that.

But the important thing is, I didn't feel as if we were doing it just because somebody pitied me. It was something we all wanted to do. It was fun—plain and simple. So I didn't feel different or small or ashamed. I didn't even feel poor. I just felt like I had some of the most awesome friends in the world.

This has probably been said a million times

before—but all the money in the world can't buy a feeling like that. And looking back, I can't even believe I made such a big deal about the money thing in the first place. But it doesn't matter. Everything worked out.

So I guess my dad's hippie stuff was right on the mark.

I should be thankful. And I am. I really am.